FOUR

BUTTONS

and

a

BASEBALL

Dennis Guzy

ISBN 978-0-578-41458-4

Acknowledgments

I would like to dedicate this book to my loving wife Marilyn who stood by me through many years, always picking me up when I was down.

To my great children Dennis and Dana, and my wonderful grandchildren. Each one inspires me in their own unique way.

To my mentor and good friend Joe Curcillo without whose invaluable friendship and assistance this book would never have been completed.

To all the men and women in our armed forces who have given their lives to our country, and to their families.

Finally, to two special friends: John Kennedy and Patrick Ghegan, United States Marine Corps, who both served in Vietnam.

Foreword

I'm glad you decided to spend a little time here in Lexiville to hear about the story we like to call *Four Buttons and a Baseball*. It's a mighty important story. Well, to us it is anyway. Now I don't want to ruin it for you, so I'll tell you this much: The story is about two heroes here in our small town, one big and one small. Both we like to think of as heroes in their own special way. I think you'll agree after you read about them.

Now I've been the official storyteller here in Lexiville for a long time. Everyone knows me as "Pops." I was born and raised here and still live in the same house my great-grandparents bought. Of course, I added plumbing and electricity along the way. This sure made going to the bathroom at night a tad easier. Now since I'm getting up there in years and may not remember every little detail I thought why not have some of the folks that were actually involved tell their part of the story. Now don't worry; I'll be here to fill in the blanks.

Chapter 1

POPS: Lexiville, USA, Summer 1967

Welcome to Lexiville. You know, 1967 was a tough time for our country what with the economy, Vietnam, and all the other things going on. We like to think that perhaps our Lexiville may have gotten frozen in time. Perhaps we could just stay the way we are, the way we were, the way we always want it to be. Well, to a certain degree it has happened. Mostly all our town residents have still lived here for generations. They're still living in the same houses just sorta passed down. Some younger ones left to find better jobs elsewhere especially when some of the factories closed. But there aren't too many houses for sale.

There's not much left for the young folk around here. Lexiville passed a zoning law that no fast-food places or other kind of junk stores could open. We have just about one of everything, but no new stores or businesses have opened recently.

You know Mickey's Diner still makes the best food around and at good prices too. Without Mickey's, who would sponsor our Little League team? *You'll never strike out when you eat at Mickey's.*

Who possibly thought of that and how could they fit all that on the team's uniform?

Well, we do have bingo on Friday at the VFW, Little League, dances, and usually something is going on around our town's gazebo.

We still have a doctor. Old Doctor Butch must have delivered every baby in this town. Some in his office, some in a car, and even a few at the hospital.

We have a vet, Doctor Mikala. She's always saying, "I'm an animal doctor, not a people doctor" to everyone who can speak who comes to her office. I think she is just as good as Doctor Butch, only her patients usually have a tail.

We also have two lawyers and they are a married couple, Bill and Linda Jones. If ever any two people were meant for each other, it was Bill and Linda. Both were local kids who, after graduating Lexiville High School, got scholarships to Penn State. They both have flaming red hair and they lived across the street from one another growing up.

When Doc Butch delivered their first baby the nurse asked Bill and Linda what they wanted to name the little girl. Bill said, "Well, you may think we're nuts, but we would like to call her Bootee. It was my mom's maiden name."

Doctor Butch thought Bill may have been overcome by the moment, but Bootee it was.

Now everyone calls her *Boots* for short and she loves it. When she was in her teens she had more colors in her hair than the rainbow. I guess Boots would be a girl you might call a tom-girl. Everyone agrees that Boots is the prettiest, kindest girl ever. She takes after her mom and dad. She even helps on bingo night. However, Boots is most popular at the VFW Friday-night dance. She makes it a point to get dressed up and she dances with every one of the veterans whose wife may have passed on. She always gives them a kiss on the cheek, a hug, and a curtsy. After dancing with Boots, old Cameron "Cami" Reyes always says, "Lord take me now, I'm ready to go." He always says that, and we always laugh. Every week.

Chapter 2

POPS: Our Story Begins

I'd like to tell you a little bit about our town as I see it if that's okay.

I rise from my bed and turn off the alarm clock at six AM. A sliver of morning sunlight passes through the thin opening of the curtains. As I open the curtains and raise the window I can feel the cool summer breeze flowing into the bedroom. "Uh, that feels so good." Another day in Lexiville, I thought, as I looked up and down our treelined street at 25 West Mercer Street where Marilyn and I have lived since we got married. As I look to the right I can easily spot the Lexiville Park where already the checkers players were mastering their trade as they have done for over fifteen years. Alongside them was the usual group of senior citizens who were caught up in no doubt a conversation about world events or who made the best hair tonic before heading up to the town square for the raising of the flag. The trees which were small saplings when planted have grown neatly and now line the park providing it with plenty of shade. I can see beyond the town square and beyond with the big gazebo right smack in the middle. I don't see many cars driving on the street. You really didn't need a car since you could walk to almost anywhere in Lexiville. Lots of folks do just that, too. There's an older couple walking hand in hand. There definitely is a lot of hand holding in Lexiville. The ice cream shoppe is just putting up the bright red umbrellas atop the outside tables. The five-and-dime store still had the "broke" note covering the coin slot of the fake rocket ship that goes up and down for a nickel. No kids would be travelling to space today. The barber shop with its red-and-white barber pole going around and round will be open in another hour or two. There's Jimmy who works at the pet store two blocks up. He's out walking the five dogs for sale or should I say they were walking Jimmy. Marilyn would buy each one of those dogs if she could.

Wait…Listen…Can you hear them? There they go right on time. The church bells playing "Amazing Grace." I always sing along. "…who saved a wretch like me." I love that song. The florist is putting out the fresh flowers. Sometimes, if I have an extra minute or two on my way to work, I'll just stop and smell them. That always makes me feel so good. All such pretty colors except there are no red roses anymore and for good reason.

Here comes the paperboy, Howie, right on time as usual. "Hello, Mr. B," Howie yells.

"Good morning, Howie," I said trying to be quiet so I don't wake up my wife Marilyn.

"Are you coming to the game tonight?" asked Howie.

"Wouldn't miss it for the world, Howie."

"And we're gonna win too, Mr. B!"

"You guys will be the champions," I said a little too loud. It was then I pulled my head in the window and banged it on the window frame. "Darn," as I reach for the lump that I know is coming. "Lucky, I have a hard head. Better keep the noise down or I will wake Marilyn." I quietly mutter to myself.

I walked down the steps and opened the front door only to see Howie has again thrown the paper in the bushes. How hard can it be to throw one rolled up newspaper in front of our door? Well, I'll say this: At least Howie is consistent. He never hits the spot he is throwing at.

But you can't help feeling sorry for Howie being adopted and all. When Howie was just a few months old his mom and dad, Doris and Dave, were going for out a night on the town. This was to be the first time since Howie was born. Let me deviate from the story just a little bit: Grandma Joan was Lexiville's babysitter back then. She didn't have a lot of money, only the government pension she got the first of each month. We all tried to help her out when we could. Jim the butcher would always add some extra meat to her order and same with Betty, the baker's wife. Grandma Joan would just march right back with the extra stuff and hand it right back. Both shopkeepers got together and agreed to say the same thing: "It's a federal law that we can't take it back, you have to keep it" So back home she went with it, her pride intact. Grandma Joan was not one to accept charity. Her husband Howard was killed in World War II and she was never quite the same after that. I think death does something to you, especially when you're not expecting it. It makes you lonely and sad and, well, every time you look around the house it's a reminder of what life used to be. Grandma Joan never moved a thing in her house except for adding the flag she was given at Howard's funeral. She kisses that flag every morning when she gets up and every night before going to bed. Sometimes she just holds it to her chest while she rocks on her rocking chair on the front porch. Whenever any of us walk by her house and see her holding that flag we never speak. We just tip our hat or maybe bow our head. We don't want to take away from the moment Grandma Joan is having.

Grandma Joan loved babysitting. The whole town would get her to babysit. Marilyn and I can't have children, but we would ask her over to mind the house while we would go for a long walk (hand-in-hand of course). It's funny, Grandma Joan always seemed to win a cash prize at bingo each week at the VFW, even at the church raffle. Well, maybe she knew things were "fixed" but just a little. Grandma Joan's hands were wrinkled, and her fingers were kinda bent inward. Doctor Butch said it was arthritis. She was always mindful of those hands. Apologizing. We always said, "Grandma Joan you have perfect baby-holding hands"

Now where were we…Oh, back to Doris and Dave. As they were getting ready to leave, Grandma Joan told them, "You youngins have a fun night on the town and don't worry about a thing."

Now you have to understand a night on the town in Lexiville is dinner at Mickey's and a drive-in movie in Bellavue the next town over. Now, you don't have to make a reservation at Mickey's, but Doris called anyway and told Mickey they would be in on Friday at five PM sharp. Mickey, knowing this was their first time out since Howie was born, put a white table cloth on the table, lit a candle and put two red roses in a vase. Mickey is just like that. Well, Doris and Dave ate their favorite dinner of liver and onions and paid their check. Mickey pinned a rose on each before they left; everyone would know they were sweethearts.

Well it was just a short drive to the Bellavue Drive-In. It was one dollar and fifty cents a car load, said the advertisement in the *Lexiville Times*, but only one dollar if you had a receipt showing you ate at Mickey's. After they parked, Dave put the big speaker on the window of their car that was half rolled down and Doris snuggled next to him. They managed to get a few smooches in before the first movie ended. Then it was time to go home. They only stayed for the first movie; they were missing Howie already.

I was told by one of the Lexiville police officers that while Dave and Doris were crossing back into Lexiville a truck was coming towards them in the opposite lane. Dave was having a hard time seeing what with those bright lights. The neighbors up the street heard the bang, an awful sound. They ran outside and saw the terrible sight. The truck had run right into the front of Dave and Doris's car killing them both. By the time the Lexiville ambulance arrived there was nothing they could do. It was hard at first to identify the bodies, but the police saw the red roses on Dave and Doris and a quick call to Mickey helped them figure out who was in the car. The state police and the coroner's office asked the ambulance crew if they could take Doris and Dave's bodies over to the Pleasant Rest Funeral Home and they did.

It was a sad time in Lexiville. Grandma Joan refused to leave their house until Dan, Dave's brother, who lived on the other side of town, could pick Howie up. She didn't want him riding in a police car. The town pulled together and we were able to get enough money for a proper burial.

Grandma Joan even went down with her government check and tried to give it to Pleasant Rest to help, but they said they already had enough.

I've never seen St. Dolan's Church filled with so many people. There were even people standing on the steps. Almost everyone in Lexiville was there. As a commemoration to the couple, everyone in the church held a red rose.

The whole altar was covered in red roses and the caskets were laying side by side, each with a red rose on top of them. The church smelled like a whole field of roses. Many of the florists from surrounding towns chipped in and helped get as many red roses as possible. Pastor Devitt spoke of the importance of life and inevitability of death. He reminded us that death can come at any time, so we should always be prepared. The pastor said he didn't know why God decided to take Dave and Doris. They were good people who had a son who would never know them. There wasn't a dry eye anywhere.

The procession of cars to the cemetery seemed to last miles. Again, police officers from the surrounding towns volunteered on their day off to come to Lexiville to help direct traffic. Our own Lexiville Police Department in their marked cars with red lights flashing were in the front, sides and rear of the line of cars which had little flags on the roof that said "Funeral, Pleasant Rest." I saw lots of people who were lined on the street put their hands over their hearts when the hearses passed by.

After the service at Saint Joseph's Cemetery, Lexiville's mayor, Karen Bestline, thanked everyone who came. She also thanked the other towns that helped. Lastly, she said that our town's florist and those of neighboring towns would no longer sell red roses in memory of Dave and Doris. The red rose would always be associated with Dave and Doris. It would always be their flower. You know what they say about a tragedy bringing everyone together.

After the funeral, Bill and Linda Jones, our town lawyers, got flooded with calls from just about everyone wanting to adopt Howie. The first offer was from Grandma Joan who was sitting on their step waiting for them to open their doors after the funeral.

Well, Dan and his wife Dottie adopted Howie and are raising him just fine along with the rest of their children. I don't think anyone has ever told Howie yet about his real mom and dad. Someone will, just not now.

Well, back to today. Ahh, the *Lexiville Times.* I opened the paper and scanned the various news articles to see if I can pick up any of the misspelled words quickly. Nine, ten...well, not too bad. Sam the typesetter must have gotten a little rest before going to work. That little one of his sure keeps him and Gretchen up a lot.

Let's see...more protesters outside the White House. I don't want to read that. Just like when I fought in Korea, it seemed like nobody back home understood what we were fighting for. Sometimes we wondered the same thing although nobody ever said anything. If that's what our country wanted, then that's what we would do.

11

Those kids ought to worry about getting a haircut instead of all this demonstrating and yelling. Well, it's almost eight AM. It's right about now that the World War II veterans will be raising the American flag in the town square.

There's not much traffic in the square at that time but everyone comes to a stop and either salutes or puts their hand over their heart when they raise the flag. Same when they bring it down at dusk. This same scene has been repeated in Lexiville for many years. There are some folks in Lexiville who may not like what's going on in our country but one thing's for sure: Everyone honors that flag.

Wow, look at the time. I got dressed and snuck back into the bedroom and quietly puts on my mailman's shirt, shorts, shoes and hat.

As I slowly closed the closet door I saw Marilyn stir a bit and as she opened her eyes she said, "Tony, why didn't you wake me? You know I love getting up with you in the morning."

"Well, I really didn't want to disturb you, you look so beautiful sleeping so comfortable. The same as the first day I married you twenty-three years ago."

"Mmm, you're sweet to say that. Let me put the coffee on for you at least."

"Already done and coffee drunk," I replied. "On my way to work; don't forget we're going to the game tonight. The Lexiville Tigers all the way."

"Do you really think they can win?" said Marilyn.

"Only if Howie learns to throw straight, honey, only if Howie learns to throw straight."

I wish the game wasn't today, I thought as I walked the four blocks to the post office. Everyone knows what today is, too. The draft notices are to be delivered today. I think I heard three for our town. Why doesn't anyone enlist? I did, and I learned a good trade.

Okay, I was a machine gunner and I still went to Korea even though I enlisted. So maybe that's not the best argument. Three is just three too many though.

Chapter 3

POPS: Draft Notices

Lexiville is still the same old town it's always been.

Lexiville is where you wanted to raise your family. Now, well, we're just like a lot of towns around here. But now we'll be sending three of our boys off to war. No, three is too many.

Pap, the postmaster of our Lexiville Post Office, greeted me as I came into the sorting area. Pap has been there for as long as anyone can ever remember. His standard greeting has never changed in all those years. "Hello, how ya'll doin'?"

"Great," I said.

Pap said, "Don't feel too good, you know what has to be delivered today?"

"Yeah, I know, I'm not happy at all about it either."

"Well it's gotta be done. Remember, I don't want you giving them to the kids. You give it to Mom or Dad, they'll give it to their sons. They know you're coming, so I suspect they'll both be there."

"It's three, right, Pap?" I asked

"Isn't that enough?"

"I'm sorry, Pap. I didn't mean it that way."

"I know you didn't, I know you didn't, it's just this darn thing has the whole town in an uproar. I don't even know what we're doing there. In World War II we knew what we were fighting for and the same with you in Korea. But here it's a place nobody ever heard of a few years back. I don't even know where to look for it on my globe. You know, I was talking with the guys this morning when we raised Old Glory and they said these boys shouldn't be going if they don't know what it's for. They even said go to Canada like everyone else. Imagine that...going to Canada. I think that's where one of those boys ought to be. Never thought I would hear something like that from them old codgers."

I finished loading my mailbag and started for the door when I said, "Pap, you going to the game tonight?"

Pap replied, "Wouldn't miss it for the world. If only that darn Howie could throw straighter, we might be able to win the championship this year!"

I laughed as I stepped out of the post office. *You won't strike out if you eat at Mickey's.* Who ever thought of that?

15

I decided to separate the three draft notices from the rest of the mail. I didn't want to get them mixed up.

Hmmm…Going to Canada...Maybe I should mention something when I deliver these. No, it's not my business to say anything. It's just like I wouldn't tell Howie's mom that Howie can't throw straight. They all will figure it out on their own.

As I spotted Miss Emma I said, "Good morning, Miss Emma!"

"Good morning, Tony, how's that lovely wife of yours?"

"Just fine, Miss Emma, Just fine."

"Going to the game tonight, Tony?"

"Yes ma'am, I wouldn't miss it for the world!"

"Do you know last week I was at the game and I almost got hit with one of those balls? I was sitting in my chair, the green-and-white one, when the next thing I know I hear 'look out!' and that ball came by me like nobody's business."

"Well how did that happen, Miss Emma?"

Then we looked at each other and said the same thing—"Howie."

"Hello, Mrs. Williams, I have something here for you. It's for Jim, but Pap told me to give it to you and the mister if he's home."

"He is, Tony, thank you and we'll give it to Jim. This darn thing has us so upset, but Jim will do whatever his country needs. Just like his daddy before him, but you know, Tony, I just don't know why it's got to be there, we never even heard of the place, Vietnam, we don't know anybody that's ever lived there or visited on vacation."

"Well, we'll see Jim before he goes. Maybe we can talk to the boys before they go, give them some pointers."

"That would be nice of you boys, real nice. Are you going to the game tonight?" Mrs. Williams said.

"Wouldn't miss it for the world. Wouldn't miss it for the world," I said a little lower as I left.

Chapter 4

POPS: Two to Go

One down, two to go.

"Good Morning, Mr. Hextall!"

"Good morning, Tony. Is that what I think it is? If so give it here. You know, Pap wouldn't even let me pick it up this morning...said you gotta deliver it. Imagine that. I can't even pick up something that says my boy Rocky has to die in some godforsaken place called Vietnam. I don't even know which Vietnam he's going to. Imagine that. Can you imagine that, Tony? I couldn't even pick it up."

"Well don't think like that, Mr. Hextall I'm sure he'll be fine."

"Is that what you think all them other fathers and mothers thought before their boys shipped out? They'll be fine. Then they didn't come home the way they left. No arm or leg, no, Tony, we don't even know why. But Rocky will go...he'll do what his government wants of him. He's no coward, he'll make Lexiville proud. You'll see."

"I'm sure he will. See you at the game tonight, Mr. Hextall?" I said.

"No, I don't think we'll be in a cheering mood tonight. I think we'll just spend it with

Rocky and, you know, just talk about things. Make sure he is all right with God and everything. I think Pastor Devitt is coming this week to speak to Rocky, too. Don't know what night."

"I'm thinking that Pastor Devitt will say the prayer before the game tonight like he always does."

"Well, he should say a prayer for that boy that can't throw straight, what's his name? Huey?"

"It's Howie, Mr. Hextall."

"Yeah well, I told Mrs. Hextall that Houdini couldn't even do a trick to make that kid throw straight. You know, that's how I remember his name Huey, Howie, Houdini, they all sound alike."

I replied, "Just like Hextall, Mr. Hextall."

"Yep I guess you could say so. Let me ask you something kind of personal if you don't mind, Tony."

"Sure, Mr. Hextall, what is it?"

"Do you think that boy maybe is cross eyed or something? You know where he threw the paper this morning? Clear over there. I told him, 'Huey, why not aim way over there at that big bush and throw the paper so then it will land right on my step?' Strangest thing I ever seen, that boy."

Chapter 5

POPS: Dutch's Draft Notice

Two down, now one to go. The hardest of all—Dutch.

"I see you got it; I've been waiting long enough for it."

"Sorry, Mrs. Blevins. Well, between these things and the game tonight I kind of got sidetracked."

"Don't worry about it, we all knew this day was coming and now it's here," said Ma Blevins."

"How's Dutch feel about it?"

"Oh, he's fine, he'll do his duty."

"Look, Mrs. Blevins, it's not really for me to say, but a bunch of us, even Pap, got together and we figure we got enough money that can get Dutch to Canada and get him on his feet. Then when this thing is done he can come home and nobody is gonna say a thing, Mrs. Blevins, nobody. We'll all see to that."

Mrs. Blevins replied, "Nobody but God, Tony. Nobody but God."

I said, "Mrs. Blevins, you know Dutch wouldn't hurt a fly. He won't go hunting. He keeps all them pets. He couldn't fight anyone, let alone kill them."

"Well maybe there's a way and, if so. God will provide it. He always has before. Now you don't pay this any mind."

I said, "Please, Mrs. Blevins, just think about the Canada part."

"Already thought about it. My Dutch is no coward and he'll do his duty like every other American boy and he'll come home to us. You hear me? He'll come home to us."

"I know, Mrs. Blevins, I know. But in what condition?"

Chapter 6

POPS: Are You Going to the Game?

"We got great seats, honey," I said to Marilyn. "What a night. Imagine our Lexiville Tigers playing in the championship." Pastor Devitt said a prayer and then the St. Joseph's choir sang the National Anthem. The American flag was presented by the Lexiville VFW Honor Guard. They even had Kirby Lantz throw out the first pitch. He lost his legs in World War II and was in a wheelchair, but he made a perfect pitch. The field looked great with the grass freshly mowed. Big Jim, Lexiville's only parks employee had laid the white chalk straight down the first base and third base lines, but he made a circle instead of a square in the batter's box. You could buy cotton candy, hot dogs, and even snow cones with five flavors, proceeds to benefit the Lexiville Tigers Athletic Association. The loudspeaker was working but it had a little hum in the background which sounded like buzzing bees.

All the players got a rousing ovation amid some of groans when the announcer said Howie was starting in center field.

"That's okay, honey. Nobody ever hits a ball that far."

And nobody had in this game; that is until the last inning with the Lexiville Tigers leading

2-1, but the Switarra "Swatties" had a runner on first and second, and boy could they run. You had to run fast when you had a uniform on that had a big fly swatter on it.

What was their slogan? *Swat now or forever hold your...*

I don't remember. Two out. Come on, strike him out and we're the champs.

This was it. Marilyn held my arm so tightly I thought my circulation had stopped. The pitcher looked, shook off the first signal, shook off the second signal...Come on, you're gonna throw the same pitch anyway.

Here it comes, the throw, and a hit...

Oh no...it drops in front of Howie in center field. Nobody ever hits it to center field. Howie caught it on one bounce; the runner on second was waved around by the third base coach and was heading for home.

It's then that Howie threw the ball as hard as he could. The ball one-hops it to the catcher who tags the runner out just before he touches the plate. "You're out!" screamed the home-plate umpire.

There was no sound, everyone was quiet. We all just sorta looked at each other with blank stares. No one could believe what they just saw. Howie, our Howie had just thrown the perfect throw and the runner was out at home plate.

The game was over, and the Lexiville Tigers had won 2 to 1. They were the champions. The first time ever. It was then that the realization had set in. Everyone started cheering and yelling. The Tigers ran out to Howie and picked him up and carried him on their shoulders. He was their hero. He was *our* hero.

The coach ran out to Howie and congratulated him giving him the game ball. "What a great throw, what a great throw... Amazing, just amazing... Howie you're gonna be the MVP," said the coach.

"But coach," Howie said. "Coach, I was throwing the ball to third base, not home."

"Shhh, Howie, that's our secret. I know."

"Oh, Marilyn, I can't believe it. What a throw by Howie. Howie, our paperboy Howie," I said.

Marilyn replied, "That sure was exciting, honey."

"Oh, Marilyn I wouldn't have missed this game for the world."

Chapter 7

DUTCH: Boot Camp

"Everybody off the bus, off the bus!" shouted the drill instructor. All the recruits rushed off the bus, some tripping over the recruit in front of them. They lined up till they were aligned with the yellow painted feet on the ground.

When all the confusion seemed to subside, and the recruits were in proper order, the drill sergeant shouted, "I am Drill Sergeant Antonio J. Pikachan. My assistant drill instructors are Assistant Drill Instructor Erik Snyder and Assistant Drill Instructor Stephen Swain."

"You will address me as *Drill Sergeant*. Do you understand?"

The recruits replied in a muffled low tone. "Yes, Drill Sergeant!"

"I can't hear you, and if I can't hear you, that must mean you don't like me," He shouted. As Sgt. Pikachan walked up and down the ranks of the new recruits he stopped in front of Dutch and asked, "Is that true soldier? You don't like me? Maybe you think my name is funny. Well, do you, soldier?"

"No, Drill Sergeant. I mean yes, I like you Drill Sergeant!" the recruit shouted.

Maybe you don't like the look of my face. Do you like my face soldier?" he said, half yelling and half spitting his words.

"No, Drill Sergeant! I mean yes, Drill Sergeant!"

"I'll be watching you, boy. I'll be watching you real close. What's your name, boy?"

"Dutch," replied the recruit.

"Uhh, Dutch. So, you and I are now on a first name basis. Is that right, Dutch? I bet you're gonna write a letter home and tell mommy you have a new best friend named Antonio."

"No, Drill Sergeant!"

A snicker could be heard from the other recruits.

"You all think this is funny? Well drop down and give me twenty push-ups. All except you, Dutch. I'm sort of taking a liking to you."

While the new recruits began their push-ups, Drill Sgt. Pikachan shouted, "I will be your mother, your father, your aunt and uncle, and even your sweet old grandmother who'll get you some warm tea when you're feeling homesick. Isn't that right, Dutch?"

"Yes, I mean no, Drill Sergeant!"

"I am going to teach you to obey orders and I am going to teach you to kill, because you are all going to Vietnam. Furthermore, the Army in their God-almighty wisdom has decided that I am going with you."

"Your training will commence tomorrow at 0600. For now, you will follow Assistant Drill Instructor Snyder where you will be issued your uniforms, equipment and bunk assignments. Also, any of you boys who may tinkle themselves at night raise your hand, so you'll be right next to the latrine."

One recruit raised his hand

"Put down that hand down, recruit. Get me that boy's name," yelled Sgt. Pikachan.

We all got in a long line and as I learned, in typical Army fashion, it was hurry up and wait. Eventually, at each station, we were given uniform shirts, pants, boots, web belts, canteens, helmets (with a piece of brown tape across the back where you wrote your name). Hardly anybody got the right size, but things seemed to work out after everyone traded with each other. The barracks room had double-stacked bunks lined along each wall. Floor lockers and wall lockers were provided for each recruit. The latrine was at the end of the hall. It wasn't home but sure was better than laying on the wet ground that we would have to get used to in Vietnam.

Chapter 8

DUTCH: We Have a Problem

"Drill Sgt. Pikachan, we have a problem"

"What sort of problem?"

"It's the new guy"

"Well, they would all seem to be new guys to me. Which new guy?"

"Blevins, Dutch Blevins. It appears that he is refusing to carry a weapon into combat and he states in his written statement here that he will not kill another human being, enemy or not."

"Is that right? I knew I had a funny feeling about Blevins. Get him in here now."

"Drill Sgt. Pikachan, recruit Blevins reporting as ordered"

Sgt. Pikachan stated, "Son, it would appear to me that we have a problem here. I'm told that you will refuse to carry a weapon in combat. Now, what do you think happens in combat son? Do you think the enemy comes up to give you a kiss or maybe he asks your okay to date your sister? Son, do you know you can be court martialed for this? If you were a conscientious objector, why didn't you state so before?"

"Permission for the recruit to speak, Sergeant," said Blevins.

"Go ahead, Blevins, this should be interesting."

"Sgt. Pikachan, I've never knowingly killed anything in my life. It's not a religious thing. It's sort of just the way I was raised. I believe in God, but that isn't the reason. If I can't give life, then I shouldn't be able to take it. I'm not a coward if that's what the guys think. I will go into war with you and those men, but I'd like to have the opportunity to save lives, not take them. When the rest of the platoon is going to Advanced Infantry Training School I'm scheduled to go to Basic Combat Medical School. I'll be here with my platoon when we ship out to Vietnam. I just don't want to carry a gun.

"Son, do you know what the life expectancy is for a medic in Vietnam? First person they shoot is the radio man. The second person is the guy talking on the radio and that would be me. Then guess who's next...you. Medics have carried guns in Vietnam since we first landed. Now, as far as if you'll carry a weapon while there. Well, we'll see. I expect you to qualify with a weapon and do everything every other recruit does while you're here. Understand? God knows we need qualified medics. First, you have to make it through my hell here at boot camp.

Many of the guys said hell would be better than boot camp. It was tough but if you paid attention and listened it wasn't that bad. There were some Vietnam veterans on the base who we got to talk to and they said what you learn in boot camp could save your life. However, the most important thing you had to do over there was pay attention and listen.

We ran everywhere or marched everywhere. We started out learning to march and ended with learning to shoot. Finally, we practiced ambush exercises. Now those were just the highlights. There was lots in between but we all made it through and graduated. My mom and dad took the bus the night before and checked into a hotel. The following day they took a cab to the base to watch me graduate. We were one proud group of soldiers. As our parents watched from the bleachers we marched across the parade ground and not one of us was out of step. Ricky Pitts carried our guidon which let the parents know what unit was marching.

Sgt. Pikachan was out in front with his sword drawn upward against his shoulder. He drew the sword up to the center of his body and turned his head slightly when we passed the flag. I was never so proud about accomplishing something as I was about this. When I met my folks afterwards I was standing between two very proud parents with Sgt. Pikachan getting our picture taken. My mom of course was crying the whole time. The last thing she said to Sgt. Pikachan was, "Please sir, bring our boy home alive."

Sgt. Pikachan replied, "Mrs. Blevins I'm gonna bring all these boys back home to their mommas alive. Don't you worry."

After graduation most of the guys went on to Advanced Infantry Training. I was sent to Basic Combat Medical School. We would all reunite afterwards and ship out to Vietnam together.

Chapter 9

DUTCH: Basic Combat Medic School

"My name is Sgt. Carter D. Sand. Welcome to Basic Combat Medic School. This course normally takes three months. However, due to the demand for platoon and squad medics, it will be condensed into a seven-day-a-week, thirty-day course. If you successfully complete this course, some of you will return to your squad or platoon if they are shipping out to Vietnam. Others will be assigned to new squads or new platoons who are already in country.

"You'll be expected to watch and learn during your deployment. God knows there's enough to learn. You will have medics who are senior to you in some cases. Watch and learn what they teach you. Doctors, nurses and surgeons in the forward battlefield locations will be more than happy to teach you. Learn from them. You are not a doctor but whatever your God-given Christian name is you most likely will be referred to as 'Doc.' It's your responsibility to look after your men. From making sure they take their pills to removing leeches to treating them for dysentery.

"At base camp and in the field, you will decide who gets evacuated and in what order. If you're still alive, that is. Every man will look to you when they need you. And need you they will, whether they are wounded by gunfire, mortar or booby traps, no matter where, you'll be there. 'DOC UP'...when you hear those words you'll move. Some, you'll be able to help, others you'll hold onto and tell them they're on the next chopper out, knowing they're gonna die.

"Some, you won't even recognize who they are. You'll look for a dog tag on a boot and wrap up what remains of them in a poncho. Just remember, it's you and only you. You freeze, you forget, you hesitate, you mess up, men will die. Your buddies will die.

"Furthermore, if you survive your year of hell in Vietnam, well, you just come on back and see your friendly old sergeant here and we can enlist you for four more years and get you the advanced training." To which there was an unmistakable groan.

"Dismissed."

After hearing that, I said to myself, "being an Army medic is where I belong"

However, after training started I wondered if I had made the right decision. There was so much to learn. Sucking chest wounds, shrapnel wounds, those who could live for a few days more and those who I thought were gonna die. I had to make that decision. I wasn't God. Who was I to decide who lived and who died? I'm just a kid from Lexiville that wanted to go on living his life and not be stuck in this hell hole called Vietnam. One thing was for sure: For the first time in my life people depended on me, Dutch Blevins. There would be no more asking my mom or dad what I should do. I made those decisions. If I brought all this responsibility on myself I better know what I'm doing. So, study I did. I aced the entire course with perfect scores. In the final practical exam, I screwed up, causing me to graduate second in my class. All because I decided not to evacuate a lieutenant colonel with trench foot. Instead, I evacuated a soldier with a shoulder wound. Well, that's the Army for you.

Chapter 10

DUTCH: Shipping Out to Vietnam

We finally made it to the airbase. I didn't know whether to feel happy or sad but today was the day and it was finally here. We were shipping out to Vietnam. I gave my mom and dad a farewell hug and kiss and heard the same advice every other mother and father was giving: Be careful, stay down and of course, don't volunteer for anything. I said all my good byes, promising my family I would write as often as I could. My mom had given me some writing paper that had different color French poodles on it. I don't think I'll be using that. My dad told me, "Dutch you don't have to return home a hero, all we want you to do is return home."

I knew there was a fairly good chance some of us may not return home, some could be missing an arm or a leg. I think that was the moment I truly realized why I was here. I was gonna take care of my guys. I started to see some of the guys from my platoon and this was the first time anyone called me 'DOC.' I reported to Sgt. Pikachan who asked me if I had changed my mind about carrying a gun. He said, "I hear you earned a marksman badge on the range? A waste of a good shot."

I saw the crew of the C-147 give a thumbs up and with that I heard the sergeant say, "Saddle Up and let's get on this bird to Vietnam."

We all lumbered aboard carrying our huge bags which contained all our stuff. Our weapons would not be distributed until we arrived in country. The plane made a few stops for gas and a flight crew change. Every time the flight crew left they all came back to wish us well. Even the ground crew that gassed us up wished us luck. We were sure getting these good luck wishes from a lot of people.

At one stop we were allowed to get off the plane and use a portable john. There was a Red Cross canteen truck there with coffee, soda, doughnuts and these small bags of pretzels. We could see down to the next hangar where there was another C-147 with its tail down and there seemed to be lots of activity with guys in their dress uniforms. Dennis asked one of the Red Cross workers, "What's going on over there, some big deals coming in?" The Red Cross worker said, "Yeah you could say that. They are getting ready to start taking off the caskets of the soldiers who were recently killed." That sort of bought everything to a halt. We decided not to run our big mouths about what we didn't know. We all stood in formation and saluted every time we saw a casket being carried down the ramp. One of the guys said, "I sure hope nobody has to do that for me."

Chapter 11

DUTCH: In Country

As Sgt. Pikachan stood before us he said, "Well men, Welcome to Firebase Michelle, here in the sunny tropical climate of Vietnam, where you are guaranteed to piss somebody off, whether it's on our side or theirs. Write your mommies and daddies and tell them you're here and you're all feeling happy. I suggest you all have a meeting with Doc Blevins about a personal decision he's made. However, not one word of this goes out of this platoon to anyone. In case you're looking for a little guidance, remember It could be your ass that's shot up when they call 'Doc Up.' Dismissed."

I stepped toward the sergeant and said, "Thanks, Sarge, for saying what you did" No telling how many of them may think I'm a coward."

Sgt. Pikachan replied, "I didn't say it for you, Blevins. I said it for them. They'll be thinking about all this once the shooting starts and everyone will curse the one man in this squad that disagreed with you especially when some half-ass replacement of yours is running in the opposite direction. No, we're not going to have disunity in this squad. God knows we'll have enough to worry about.

At about 1800 hours I got together with the guys from my squad and explained to them my rationale for not carrying a weapon . A lot of them had questions and I answered them all. One of the final things I said was "When you hear the words 'Doc Up' look forward, because that's where I'll be heading." Finally, I told them if they didn't want me in the squad I would ask for a transfer, but I wanted to be with them. I let them talk on it for a while as I made my way to the supply hut.

When I came back I saw they were still all lingering around.

Then, Private Jeff Trotman who, as he liked to say, is a hell-raiser from the Keystone State of Pennsylvania, stepped forward and said, "the guys in the squad asked me to be their spokesman, so here I go. Not one of us is against you staying with the squad, Dutch. We all thought of it kind of differently. Maybe, if a man wants to risk his own life by not carrying a weapon to save another person's life, that says a lot about that person. He sure ain't a coward. A little bit nutty maybe, but ain't nobody here thinks you're a coward. We know when we hear 'Doc Up' that you're gonna be moving up to where you're needed. Hopefully you and Sgt. Pikachan can get us all home alive."

It looks like I just convinced the members of my squad of the seemingly impossible.

It was right about then that Sgt. Pikachan came by and said, "All right, it's settled. Everybody in this squad has a job to do and we're gonna do it. Get some sleep; we'll meet at the operations tent at 0500, and 0530 we're off on our first mission. Let's bring some of that Keystone State hell to this corner of Vietnam. Dismissed."

Back in our hooch Dennis and I had a real in-depth conversation. We talked about the war, our folks back home and what may happen if we get killed over here. We both believed in God and there is a mighty fine Chaplain here. They told me his name was Captain John Kennedy and he even went out on extended patrols with some of the squads, although the top brass here don't like it.

As I was thinking about tomorrow I said, "Well, Dennis, I guess this is where we pray."

"Dutch, I started praying last night. Just think, we have 364 and a wake up," said Dennis. "You scared, Dutch?"

"Scared as all get out," I said.

"What do you think it's gonna be like?"

"Well I don't think it's gonna be like in the movies, that's for sure. I think like Sgt. Pikachan said we just gotta rely on our training and listen to him and whoever else we're with. This place isn't like I thought it would be though.

I mean it stinks. You can't really trust some of the Vietnamese villagers because they might be the enemy. We don't speak the same language. They don't even fight like we do. They hide in holes in the ground, shoot and then run away."

Dennis said, "I hope I get me lots of medals, so I can show them off when I get home. Man, the girls in my town would love seeing a guy in a uniform with lots of medals I bet. They all will be saying you're a hero."

"I don't want to be a hero, Dennis, I just want to do what I promised to" said Dutch.

Dennis replied, "yeah, Dutch, I think you're right. One thing I don't wanna be is a coward and that's what I'm afraid of. When the shooting starts what if I freeze up? What if I piss my pants or throw up?"

"Well Dennis, I can only say if that happens you're gonna have a sore backside because there's gonna be a lot of guys kicking you in the butt, starting with Sgt. Pikachan."

Dennis thought about it a minute and said, "Well, I just don't want to be thought of as a coward that's all. Can you imagine our folks back home getting told that? I don't know where you're from, but I come from a small town and it would be all over town it in no time."

"Let me ask you a question, Dutch. Do you think any of those soldiers in those caskets were cowards? I mean, you can't be a coward and dead, right?"

"You know, that's a good question. I would think that a coward would be someone who didn't do his duty or who ran to the rear or left his squad, slept on guard watch or didn't help another soldier that needed it. I'm not looking to be anything special here neither a coward or a hero. I just want to be plain old Dutch and go home to Lexiville. But you gotta promise that when we get back that you'll come down and visit. My folks would like you, you know that? They would really like you."

"Probably best not to think too much more about it now. Let's get some sleep. See ya in the morning."

I prayed for everyone in our squad that we would make it home okay. I prayed the same prayer every night until one night I stopped praying it.

Chapter 12

DUTCH: First Combat Mission

0530, Helicopter Pad.

We checked and rechecked our gear as we prepared to board the Hueys. The helicopter pad seemed like controlled chaos. Lots of guys running around, fueling the choppers, loading ammunition for the door gunner's M60s. It smelled like a gas station from back home. The sound was deafening, and dust was blowing all around. It sure was a site to see as those Hueys had flown into the firebase in formation. It seemed that a lot depended on these chopper pilots and I have to say they are some of the bravest men I know. Even the crew chief and door gunner wouldn't hesitate to help load our wounded or dead, exposing themselves to enemy fire. I still could never understand how the VC or NVA could have known where we were gonna land. It seemed like every landing zone was hot.

After we took off we made two false insertions; they were just miles from the LZ. They had already hit the place with artillery for twenty minutes and the escorting gunships were now shooting up the tree line with their M60s

The Huey hovered just a few feet off the ground as the men either jumped or fell off the chopper. It took off quickly and hovered above as the men made their way to the tree line. Wow, that wasn't too bad, I thought, just as a mortar shell exploded in a tree above us, showering us with dirt and branches.

Sgt. Pikachan yelled, "Let's go, move out, they got us zeroed in here!" Our guys made their way along an adjacent trail, carefully watching the terrain for booby traps. Our point man made frequent stops to listen. Just then a shot rang out and everyone hit the ground. Just one shot, but who fired? The answer came quickly as I heard "Doc Up." Well, this is it, I thought. My baptism of fire. When I arrived I saw Ricky Pitts, the radioman, was shot just above the shoulder blade. There was little blood.

"Looks like we got us a sniper out there, so everyone keep low," said the sergeant. "Corporal, take three men and scout the area and see if you find this S.O.B. and we'll reign artillery down on their ass."

"How's he looking, Doc?" asked the sergeant.

I examined the wound. "Not bad. Through and through, good enough for a Purple Heart, not good enough for a medivac, although I'll keep an eye on it for infection. I think somebody else needs to carry the radio though." After I finished bandaging Pitts, it dawned on me that that's who Sgt. Pikachan said would get shot first. I wonder what he's thinking now? I worked up a sling for Ricky after we got the radio off his back.

The men returned from looking for the sniper; they couldn't find him.

"All right, move out," said the sergeant. The rest of the squad knew that they could be the next one shot without even knowing where it came from. Seems like my stock just rose a little bit.

I was always writing my folks, so I finally had to resort to using the poodle paper from my mom. In the last letter from my mom she wanted to know more about where we lived and what kind of food we ate. So I wrote back, *Well, we live in hootches (really tents), each tent holds about four guys. It has four bunks and lockers but that's it. Nothing homey about it. They say it's better that way in case you know one of your buddies who "gets it." The mess tent food is okay although sometimes it seems everybody gets diarrhea at the same time. Out in the field it's K-rations. Plus we are upwind of the latrine which is a definite benefit but only two tents away from the mess hall where the rats seem to congregate. Mom, I've seen some big rats here. We bought a cat from one of the Vietnamese kids figuring that would help, but a rat ate it. The cat was probably gonna get eaten anyway just the rat got to it first. We dug a trench around the outside, so the rain water would run off, but it didn't take long for those just to fill up with water. Those rats were awfully good swimmers. They could go around the hooch maybe four or five times before they started to slow down. Then they would just jump out and head back towards the mess tent. After seeing all those rats, I know why the guys don't make fun of the cooks. They are really all nice guys just trying their best to finish their twelve months like us.*

Our squad had remarkably good luck over the next few months. The monsoons had curtailed patrolling except for in and around the firebase. A few minor gunshot wounds, some punji-stake booby traps and some malaria and dysentery cases, but all in all, our nine months in country thus far had gone far better than we expected. However, Intelligence had reported the NVA and the VC were setting up more ambushes to make up for the lull in activity during the monsoon rains.

When my mom heard about all the rain she decided to send me a bright-yellow plastic raincoat and some rubbers or, as some others may call them, galoshes. She assured me that this would keep me dry. Unfortunately, I didn't think the Army would approve of my new foul-weather gear. But that coat and those rubbers kept a lot of things dry back in our hooch. The guys got to storing their extra cigarette packs in the rubbers. We had told the Vietnamese in the camp they were booby trapped to keep them from rooting around in our hooch when we were out on patrol.

I continued writing home during my time in country ensuring my mom and dad of our platoon's good fortune. That good fortune was just about to change, however.

Like so many other squads who were beginning to think of being a "short-timer" we started to grow lax. Sgt. Pikachan knew we were not a sharp as when we arrived. He constantly drilled, redrilled, trained, retrained, shouted, threatened and everything else he could think of. It didn't matter, and despite hearing about a lot of short-timer horror stories things didn't really change. We had two months left in Vietnam and we felt invincible.

Chapter 13

DUTCH: Ambush the Ambushers

Sgt. Pikachan had just returned from an intelligence briefing. He called us together and told us to prepare for a four-day patrol tomorrow. We would leave at first light by chopper, traveling several klicks beyond our firebase. However, we would be well within our artillery umbrella; also, we would have air and helicopter support. This was to be a search-and-destroy mission. The plan was to surprise the North Vietnam ambushers who had been operating inside our area. The patrol included Sgt. Pikachan, Trotman, Radioman Pitts, Dennis, me, an Air Force FAC (Forward Air Controller) named Doug, and a Kit Carson scout.

Every member of our patrol had checked and rechecked their weapons except me. I inspected my medical supplies trying to think if there was anything else that may be needed. We boarded the Hueys feeling almost morose. After a few false insertions, we landed on an open patch of ground and quickly moved to the tree line. We moved several klicks into the bush and set up for a night ambush. We set our Claymore mines along the trail. We confirmed with Firebase Michelle that they were at the correct coordinates. Now we settled in the tree line along the trail and waited.

Because of the severity of the intel reports, Sgt. Pikachan had everyone at one-hundred-percent alert. At about 0500 Pitts thought he heard movement. He took off his radio and moved forward of his position when he saw a VC clad in black pajamas moving up the trail haphazardly. Pitts thought capturing a prisoner would be helpful in learning more about these ambushes so he moved from his position just as the VC ran back up the trail with Pitts running after him. The next thing you know, Dennis ran off in pursuit of Pitts.

In the meantime, Sgt. Pikachan returned from rechecking the ambush position when his worst fears came true: The radio was on the ground, Pitts and Dennis were gone, and the crack of AK-47 fire along with that of a machine gun filled the air. Pikachan said, "Come on, Doc, I think we're gonna need you." He told the FAC who had grabbed the radio to start setting up artillery and air support as there may be trouble ahead. As Pikachan and I ran to just short of the clearing we both saw Pitts and Dennis laying on the ground bleeding profusely. I ran forward zig-zagging back and forth and I crouched behind their bodies. I was trying to patch them up but there was blood all over. Dennis had been shot through his helmet and part of the back of his head was a few feet away. I reached out and grabbed it and put it on Dennis's chest. I could see he was hardy breathing and then his eyes rolled back. I knew there was nothing more I could do.

I crawled over to Pitts, the whole time bullets pinged around me. Pitts had been shot three times, twice in the upper chest and once in his hand that still held on to his M16. Pitts kept telling me to go back. I methodically started patching the wounds with gauze, but Pitts kept on bleeding. Then, Pitt's body seemed to stiffen and then went limp. I knew he was the second friend I had lost.

Sgt. Pikachan laid down covering fire yelling for me to return. I started trying to drag my two friends back but the whole time bullets were flying. There was loud shouting and the next thing I knew a grenade rolled right towards Dennis's body. I hugged the ground. The grenade exploded. Dennis had taken most of the shrapnel, but I was hit in my leg. I looked back to where I could hear someone yelling my name and the next thing I saw was Sgt. Pikachan running towards me firing his M16.

Pikachan fell just a few feet from me and I could see that blood was spurting from a neck wound. I reached over and pulled Pikachan towards me. I laid on top of his body to shield him as best I could. I put my hand over Pikachan's neck trying to slow the bleeding. It was no use. There was so much blood. The sight and smell was more than I could have ever imagined. I could see that Pikachan's face was dull white as blood continued to spurt from his wound. His chest didn't move. I yelled, "Sarge, tell me what to do, tell me what I gotta do."

Pikachan didn't answer. I grabbed his hand and said, "Don't worry Sarge, you're going out on the first medevac." It seemed like an eternity had passed but it was just a few seconds.

I heard loud screaming and yelling. I looked up to see six, no seven, Viet Cong running directly towards me each firing wildly.

I knew what I had to do. Pikachan told me what I had to do. KILL THE ENEMY. Without thinking I picked up the M16 next to Sgt. Pikachan and on full auto sprayed the attacking Viet Cong, killing them all. It was then I realized that I had been wounded in the groin and was losing blood fast. I felt like my leg had been hit with a baseball bat. The pain was unbearable, and it felt as if my leg was on fire. I tried to move it, but I couldn't. If only I could pull the bodies back. These were my friends. I promised to protect them. Sgt. Pikachan and I were gonna get them all home safely. Now three of them were dead. It was my fault. I laid on top of Pikachan's body to shield him from any further bullets. "You're going out on the first chopper, Sarge" I kept repeating. As I laid there I thought: I'm a failure. That was the last thing I remembered and then I passed out.

Chapter 14

DUTCH: You're a Hero

As I started to wake I could hear the call: "Doc up." I instinctively looked for my medical bag, which was soaked in blood. "Hey Buddy, man, you just lay there, Doc's on the way up. I thought you were dead. I was ready to call in an airstrike on this whole area to get them all, but you did a pretty good job yourself. You're a hero, man," said the FAC. "I saw you move a little, but we had to wait for the reaction force from the firebase till we could move out to check you."

"What about the others—Ricky and Dennis. My sergeant?" I asked.

"Sorry man. They're dead; they walked right into the ambush. They never had a chance. Pikachan was trying to get to you when he got it. Man, why were you trying to drag the bodies back?"

"They were my brothers, all of them," said Dutch.

"Just stay still, man. Doc is on the way over"

Chapter 15

DUTCH: Grab Me the Buttons

I said to the FAC, "Could you grab a button off of each of their jackets and one off mine?"

"Yeah, you sure that's all you want is a button? Maybe you could notch the first letter of their name on it. Looks like I'm gonna be here for a while till the dust-off gets here or until I die first."

"You ain't gonna die, Dutch," said Doc Rob Cannish. "That's why they sent me, the best there is, next to you, of course. But this your ticket home, buddy boy. You did it, you survived Vietnam. Plus, you're a hero."

"ME?" I said. "I'm no hero."

"You ought to hear what the FAC is saying. You ran over to the first two guys that were hit, apparently realized they were dead, then ran over to your sergeant, covering him with your body while taking out six of theirs. You're a hero, Dutch. We got a dust-off en route. Got a tourniquet on you. You're patched up for now, but I told them to get the surgeons on alert when you get back to our base camp."

"What those guys were saying about me...I'm no hero. Please tell them that," I said.

"Okay, whatever. Guys, over here! Get him in a poncho and get him on the chopper. Sorry Dutch, but we have to fly you out with the dead guys in your squad," said Doc Cannish.

As I was loaded in the medevac I heard a voice say, "Hold up." It was the FAC. "Here, I got those buttons for you. All three. I marked them, and I put them in an envelope with a letter to my wife. I told her not to worry, I was safe and sound. Don't forget to take them out. Could you see that gets in the base mail?"

"Sure, thanks," I said.

As I looked over at the sergeant, Ricky and Dennis I saw that all three of their top buttons had been ripped off. The bottom ones were covered in blood. I reached inside my jacket and took out the envelope. I opened it and ripped off the top button off my jacket and added it to the envelope. Now there were four buttons. I held onto Sgt. Pikachan's hand the whole way back. I felt like I was a coward; maybe if I carried a gun, maybe if I got to the guys faster, maybe I should have went back when Sgt. Pikachan had yelled for me. They were all dead now. No, I ain't no hero, I thought to myself. I'm a coward.

Chapter 16

DUTCH: The Nightmare Begins

I know that I had passed out during the rest of the chopper ride. The next thing I knew I was waking up with bright lights in my eyes and people cutting off my clothes.

"Wait a minute, what are you doing?" I asked.

"Sit back, soldier. We're gonna take care of you," said a nurse wearing surgical scrubs. You're in the rear at a surgical hospital. You've been wounded pretty bad but we're gonna take good care of you."

I felt a stab in my forearm and immediately began to relax as the IV started pushing morphine into my body.

"I have something important to ask you," I said. "Very Important."

"If it has anything to do with asking me out on a date, the answer's NO," said the nurse.

"No, no... it's not that. I have an envelope in my shirt pocket. The buttons in there are important to me. I need to keep what's inside."

"Okay, let me look. Here it is. A letter to your wife with four buttons in it. So that's why you didn't ask me out?"

I said, "No, no. The letter is not mine. It's a guy that was with us. I asked him to take some buttons from some of the guys from my squad who were killed. I need them. They can't get lost."

The nurse answered, "I'm sorry...I didn't realize that. I will make sure that they're safe. My name is Lt. Christina Cannester. I'm going to write it down and have it attached to your chart."

Dutch said, "Ma'am, has anyone ever told you that you look like an angel, a princess?"

"More like a devil," said the nursing supervisor, Esther "MAC" Ardle.

Christina answered, "Yes they have, thank you. Like an angel or a princess. You better remember this for later but for right now, it's nighty-night."

My mind went hazy and before you know it, I was out cold, and the hard work began as the trauma surgeons looked around trying to decide where they were going to start. The head surgeon, Maj. Terry Davis, said, "Luckily this guy's a medic, or the doc who tended to him was a good medic, because without these tourniquets he would have bled out a long time ago. Well let's see if we can save his leg and thigh... it's a real mess."

When I awoke I was in pain from my head to my toes. I had all kinds of things attached to or running into my body. I felt under the covers and my leg was still there, but I couldn't move it. Thank God. Just then I saw Nurse Christina.

"You know, you really do look like a princess." I said with a smile.

"Okay, how's my favorite patient? I just stopped in to see how you're doing? You look a lot better than when you came in. Keep up that charm. You're saying all the right things, but for now I have to get back to the operating room. We have more incoming."

"The buttons?" I anxiously asked.

"In your chart it says that there is an envelope attached and it has your buttons."

I asked, "Are you sure they're safe?"

Christina said, "They're safe. We caught the button thief last week."

"Thanks for taking care of me and the buttons. You are so pretty. I never had a girlfriend, you know?"

"What was wrong with the girls in your town?" asked Christina.

"There weren't enough of them," I said.

I know I spoke more and more with Nurse Christina about the buttons and their importance to me.

"Dutch, I have a feeling that once you can let go of these buttons, your grief is gonna end. Give them to someone that you care about. Let them honor your friends and free your conscience. I'll look on you later, Dutch, and maybe we can talk more," she said. I never saw Christina again.

I was transferred from ward to ward and sometimes was housed with guys who were hurt a lot more than me. I wrote my parents and told them not to worry about me, I would make a full recovery. I think that was the first time I ever knowingly lied to my folks.

Eventually, I got the good news that I was going to be flown back to the United States. When that day came I left with happiness and sadness. When I got better I was going to try and contact Sgt. Pikachan's, Dennis's and Ricky's folks and tell them what happened. I know I would have to admit that I was a coward and maybe I could have prevented their deaths. I had no idea what their reaction to that would be.

I shipped my uniform and all my gear back home. I didn't know how long I was going to be here.

I never told my mom and dad exactly what happened. All they were ever told was from the casualty officer that came to the house. As my mom wrote in a letter, she sorta fell and my dad thought her heart had stopped so he got Doc Butch on the phone. Doc Butch called the Lexiville Ambulance to take her to the hospital where he met them. The casualty officer was kind enough to drive my dad over to the hospital, but my mom turned out to be okay. Okay for a mom whose son was all shot to heck and could hardly move one side of him. The casualty officer, I think they told me his name was Warrant Officer J.N. Tee, stayed with my dad all day and night at the hospital till my mom was released. He drove them home.

He told my folks that he was wounded in Vietnam, too. He was a helicopter pilot and flew into a hot LZ to deliver some ammo and water to a platoon that was ambushed. He also had fly out the dead and wounded. As soon as the skids hit the ground the door gunner started throwing out the ammo and water jugs as the guys came running up with two dead and four wounded. After they got loaded on board he started taking off and just then a VC came out of the brush directly in front of him and started shooting into the canopy with his AK-47. He got hit in the arm and the hand but was still able to take off. As he was just a few feet in the air a bullet grazed off his helmet knocking him out. The chopper hit the ground hard. The door gunner couldn't swing his gun around to the front, so he jumped out and shot the VC with his .45. In the meantime, the crew chief had yanked the pilot's seat quick-release rod which caused the seat to fall backwards. With his hands now off the controls the co-pilot took over and was able to get them out of there. Those pilots were the bravest men I ever knew. They were real heroes. I can never remember them refusing to fly into a hot LZ to bring us ammo and water and take out the wounded. The gunships would fly above and would shoot their rockets into spots we identified with colored smoke. The only problem with that was the VC had taken some of the smoke grenades off a dead GI and would throw the same color into our positions.

I remember my dad telling me mom had made some tea and bought out the Howdy Doody cookie jar with homemade peanut butter and ginger snap cookies. After hearing that story, they thought the same thing was gonna happen again to my mom. She started to sway a bit from side to side. I guess maybe because the letters I wrote then told a sorta different story about what was going on over there. I didn't want them to worry about me. The casualty officer told my folks to be patient with me and I may not come home the same way as when I left. War changes people, especially if they've been wounded or had friends wounded or killed. He wrote down his office and home phone number and was always there whenever my folks had a question. He was a real hero. He called me at the hospital a few times to talk to me, but I always told the nurses to tell him I wasn't there. I never called him back. I guess I was embarrassed. I wished I would have talked to him and thanked him. I never did though. I really wished I would have. I heard later that he was buried with full military honors at Arlington National Cemetery. I think that's where I'd like to be buried. God, those chopper pilots were brave guys. Really brave guys.

My folks assured me that they would provide whatever support they could, but I got the feeling they just couldn't understand exactly what I was saying in my letters. I wanted to tell them the full story, but I was ashamed.

There were tons of times that they said they wanted to come to see me. I told them no. I made an excuse that it was too long of a drive for my dad, so they said Tony would drive up. I said no to that. My mom said they could take a train. No, no, what didn't they understand? I didn't want them to see me like this. I couldn't walk without crutches or a cane. If I fell over I couldn't get up. But, you know, just like in Vietnam guys would get out of their beds or nurses would come running to help me. You know a lot of those guys were hurt way more than me. Some of them were even married and had kids. What was life going to be like when they got home?

I think maybe I was using the hospital as a crutch. Like in Nam in a defensive position, three guys would lay face down spread out in a circle with our legs touching, that way we could see all around and no one could get in our circle. I knew I couldn't stay there forever. Sooner or later I would have to face the reality of going home or going somewhere where maybe nobody knew me.

Chapter 17

DUTCH: I Gotta Get Out of Here

Like I said before, as soon as I arrived back into the States I wrote my folks and asked them not to come visit me. I was in bad shape and I'm not sure how my mom would take it. Plus, I still couldn't resolve in my head what happened and what I did or didn't do that caused my three friends to die.

I received an honorable discharge and was awarded numerous medals. I didn't want any special award ceremony. Plus, the Army saw fit to grant me a seventy-five-percent service-related disability. I lucked out in that the Army would continue to care for me since my injuries were service related.

Finally, the day came when I couldn't take it no more. I had to get out. I would do anything to get out.

I asked Doc Womper, "How many more surgeries to go? I can't take this no more. I want to go home."

Doc Womper replied, "Dutch, you just have to be patient with us. We just can't cure all the damage done to your thigh and leg overnight. Think of it like building blocks. We can't start the next part till we've finished the first part. We've been treating the pain as best we can, but I fear you may be a bit addicted, so in time we're gonna have to slow you down on that."

I said, "Then will the pain go away with more operations and you giving me less pain meds?"

"No, Dutch, it means you're going to have to start dealing with it yourself."

"There's a lot I can't deal with."

Doc Womper said, "Look, Dutch, you're starting to get up and move around a little. Show me and the physical therapists that you'll be willing to give it a real go and maybe we can get you back home for a month or so."

I attended the mandatory meetings with the hospital psychiatrists to talk about the death of friends in Vietnam and how to deal with it. Also, they explained the antiwar demonstrations that were taking place all over the United States.

I did everything I could to get out. I attended all his meetings, met with my peer group and my personal psychologist assigned by the hospital. It didn't matter at all. I had no intention of ever returning.

When that day finally arrived, I reached into my pocket and found the most important thing of all—the envelope with the four buttons in it. I hobbled out in street clothes on a thirty-day medical leave home. My folks had already sent me money for the train.

Chapter 18

HOWIE: The Gazebo

My dad was sorta like a handyman. He was a carpenter, plumber, electrician, roofer and who knows what else he did. He just had a knack for learning from anyone willing to teach him. It was only two years ago when my dad retired. That was just when the hat factory closed.

Everybody in Lexiville would call him to fix this or fix that. I got to go along and be his helper. The pay was bad, nothing really except maybe an ice cream cone on the way home. My dad wouldn't take money from folks if they didn't have it. Said it wasn't right.

So, one day the mayor and some of the folks on the town council said, "Jake, we want to hire you." Of course this was funny since his real name was Dan. They said, "We want you to build us a gazebo in the center of town. Big enough so the whole town band can play in there. We want you to paint it white with red and blue trim."

Well, with the help of a lot of volunteers, all who knew or even didn't know about gazebo building, showed up to help. I can still remember some of the seniors sitting in their lawn chairs yelling advice. I once told my dad I thought it was leaning a bit to the right. I still think it does but maybe it's my eyes or something. Some would get there even before my dad, so they could tell him everything he did wrong before he even started for the day. It took one whole summer, but it was the best gazebo any town had. If you can picture this: a gazebo right smack in the middle of Lexiville. It was huge, it was painted white, the floor was painted blue and the posts that rose up from the floor were painted red. It had little benches on the inside to sit on, and lights on the inside that would stay on till nine o'clock.

After it was done the VFW held a turkey raffle which Grandma Joan won, and the VFW put up a giant flag pole. Next to it they put these real nice white stones around it. Since our school was just around the corner, sometimes our teachers would take us there to say The Pledge of Allegiance or we would learn all about the flag. All year long there was something going on there. The Lexiville band would play and some of the ladies would sing. They had pumpkin carving at Halloween, at Christmas they had a manger scene in there. On Christmas Eve Pastor Devitt would hold an outdoor service and people would dress up like Mary and Joseph and they also had a real live baby in the manger. My dad used to joke and say the only thing missing was the three wise men who couldn't be found in Lexiville. It had lots of garland, red poinsettias and white twinkle lights. We all sang Christmas carols and drank warm cider. Why, some people even got married in there. It looks as good today as the day my dad built it. Lots of towns have gazebos but this one the best and I'm not just saying it just because my dad built it. Well, he did have all those helpers plus me.

Chapter 19

POPS: Dutch's Homecoming

I drove two hours to pick up Dutch up at the train station. Dutch's mom and dad stayed behind wanting to make sure everything at the Gazebo was right. They wanted this to be the perfect homecoming for their son.

When Dutch got off the train I was surprised by what I saw. Dutch wasn't wearing his uniform. In fact, he was wearing ragged jeans and an old Army jacket tied with rope. His face looked old and his hair was dirty. It looked like he hadn't shaved in weeks.

I said, "Well look at you Dutch, aren't you a sight for sore eyes?"

"Yeah, a real sight, Tony. I can hardly walk; I need pain killers to keep me going from day to day. All my buddies who I was supposed to protect are dead and I said I'd never kill anyone. My sergeant said I wouldn't have to kill anyone, but they're all dead, Tony. All dead."

I said, "Dutch, why not talk to Pastor Devitt. He'll be at your house. Your folks and the town are throwing you a little welcome home party. Please, Dutch, you must talk about stuff like this. Don't let it get to you or it will destroy you inside. You'll never be the same again."

Dutch said, "I don't want to think about what a failure I am, what a coward I am. You know it. My folks know it. Christina knew it. The whole town knows it. Throw me a party. What...to laugh at me? Dutch the coward. Yeah, laugh it up, look at Dutch."

Just a few miles before Lexiville there were four Lexiville police cars with their lights and sirens on that seemed to surround my car. "What's going on?" said Dutch.

I replied, "That's your official police escort to Lexiville, Dutch"

Dutch could see all the yellow ribbons tied around anything big enough to hold a ribbon.

Dutch said, "Tony I don't want all this, I don't deserve all this. I'm no hero. Don't they know what happened?"

I said, "Dutch, whatever happened there you are a hero to your mom and dad and to every person in Lexiville."

As we arrived we could see the whole town turned out to greet Dutch. The first thing Dutch saw was the gazebo. It was decorated with red, white and blue streamers and lots of yellow ribbons. It looked beautiful. The Lexiville High School Marching Band was playing some Sousa marches. The VFW lined up and was ready to make him an official member. The mayor had the key to the city. Pastor Devitt, Pap, there were so many faces, but it was too loud, too loud, thought

69

Dutch. He saw lots of happy faces smiling and grinning and people were slapping him on the back, but it was too loud. Children were running in and out of the gazebo. The fire trucks turned on their flashing lights and tapped the sirens. Dutch started feeling strange, like he had to get away. His rage was starting to build. Don't they know I'm a coward, a failure? They're laughing at me, thought Dutch. My three buddies are dead because of me. Do they know that?

Howie patiently waited for Dutch's arrival. He could hear the sirens coming closer and closer. He held on to his baseball tight. He wanted to show Dutch the ball from the game when he was a hero.

Dutch and I got out of the car and I ushered Dutch to the middle of the town square. When Dutch's mom and dad saw him, they ran to him. His mom kissed him, and his dad saluted him. The *Lexiville Times* took a picture intending to put it on the cover of the next day's newspaper. Howie approached Dutch and said, "Hi, Mr. Dutch, I'm Howie and I want to show you the ball from the game."

Dutch just passed right by Howie, banging in to him and causing him to drop the ball. Howie picked it up and said, "Hi, Mr. Dutch. My name is Howie and you're my hero. I want to show you my ball from our…"

With that Dutch stopped, looked at Howie, and said, "Look kid, I'm not your hero or anybody's hero. If you're looking for a hero go look elsewhere, okay?" With that Dutch brushed by Howie like he wasn't even there.

Howie's mom and dad quickly grabbed him sensing something was wrong. They told Howie, "I think this is all a bit much for Mr. Dutch, maybe we can all visit him in a few days and you can show him your ball." Howie started to cry as he put the ball back in his pocket.

Dutch said, "I don't want this. Leave me alone, please." Then Dutch's mom tried to take his Army jacket off him. It was all ragged. He had ripped all the buttons off and had tied it with a rope.

Dutch's mom said, "Please Dutch, let me fix your coat when you get home. It's so old and raggedy, are you sure you just don't want to throw it away?"

"No, no, no," said Dutch. "Please Mom, let me be" said Dutch. His mom said; "Dutch maybe you could go home and get out of these ratty clothes and put on your nice uniform."

Dutch knew they finally figured it out. He backed away. They all wanted him to be the hero he knew he wasn't. It was all just a show. He was nothing more than a coward dressed in a raggedy coat.

Maybe that's was why my mom wanted the coat, so she could throw it out, maybe burn it so nobody would know. Dutch had to get out of there. He asked me if he could borrow my car. I said sure. Dutch took the bag of belongings the hospital had sent along and what little money he had. He jumped in my car and started driving. He decided to drive until he ran out of gas, and that's where he would stay, and that's exactly what he did. As the engine sputtered he pulled the car off to the side of the road. He got out and put a note under the windshield that said, "out of gas."

Dutch thought that would buy him a few more days before the police figured out whose car it was. Dutch would be long gone by them. And he was.

Dutch started hitchhiking. Lots of cars passed him, probably too scared to pick up a guy that looked like him. Finally, an older guy in a beat-up pick-up truck stopped and said, "Where you going, feller"

Dutch said, "As far as you'll take me." The old timer told Dutch to hop in.

There wasn't much conversation for the first few minutes, but the driver started out, "Were you in the Army? That looks like an Army coat."

"Yeah," said Dutch.

The old timer said, "My son was in the Army. Maybe you know him."

"I don't know him," said Dutch.

"Well, how would you know if I ain't told you his name? Okay then, let me ask you this: Were you in Vietnam?"

Dutch replied, "Yeah, I was in Vietnam"

"Okay, so was my boy. He was a hero, so I thought you may have known him."

Dutch was getting angrier. "I told you I don't know him."

"Well, I guess not then. He never made it home. He was killed."

Dutch said, "I'm sorry. I didn't know that. How did it happen?"

"Doesn't much matter, dead is dead. He's gone. Now all we can do is visit his grave, look through our photo albums. We left his room the same as when he left. You know he got engaged before he left, that poor girl. Don't matter now though, dead is dead."

"What was his name?" asked Dutch.

"Doesn't matter any, dead is dead, and you said you didn't know him. I'm getting off at this exit, so I'll drop you off."

As Dutch was opening the door he repeated, "What was your son's name?"

The driver replied, "Dead is dead, and you didn't know him."

Dutch was angry at himself. He thought maybe he just wanted to get it off his chest about his son being in Vietnam too. *I didn't take the time to listen to him.* Dutch would learn that not having anyone listen to the whole story would haunt him for a long time. Dead is dead. Dutch started to cry as he thought of himself again as a failure for not talking to that dad, that special dad. Ricki's dad, Dennis's dad, Sgt. Pikachan's dad. He could have been one of their dads.

Dead is dead.

Chapter 20

DUTCH: A New Beginning

Well, this is it. Nobody knows me here. They don't know that Dutch the coward is here. People sure look at me funny. It must be my Army jacket tied up with the string. Maybe they thought I stole it. I don't care.

Dutch soon found out that life was a bit hard living on the street. But he was able to make do. There was a mission where he could eat and sometimes find some decent clothes. There were other vets at the mission. They tried to talk to Dutch, but Dutch wasn't interested. He kept to himself.

He could sit outside the market and ask for money, and if nobody complained, they wouldn't chase him. Dutch was always respectful to the police and they kind of kept an eye out for him. People that lived there sure were different. It seemed like everybody was in a hurry all the time. Thanksgiving would be here soon, and Dutch hoped he could get a turkey dinner at the mission.

Things started to be a lot clearer in his mind. The four buttons. Why did he get them to start with? Why did he keep them? They were the only link to the men he failed, the men who depended on him, the men who died. He would be forever tied to those memories with those buttons. Back when he was in the hospital, the "nut" doctor told him that once he got rid of those four buttons his guilt would be gone. Not likely to happen, thought Dutch. Not now, not ever. Besides, whenever he touched those buttons he didn't feel like a coward anymore. He felt something special when he held those buttons. Dutch couldn't understand it. It was almost like he was getting a feeling of, *let go, Dutch, let go*. He was more confused than ever. He had to think this through.

Maybe like nurse Christina said, find someone who you could pass their memory on to. That would help you honor your friends and that would also help to take away some of your guilt. These had to be good people, selfless people. He would know them when he met them. If he ever did.

Chapter 21

DANA: Life Changes

Our family is having our usual Thanksgiving feast this year, as always.

I can remember Mom doing her last-minute shopping for our turkey and all the trimmings, when we stumbled upon a homeless man begging outside the store.

Now, we have seen him before, and despite feeling sorry for him, Mom never let us give him any money because she thought it would just go for drugs or booze. Plus, he was dirty, smelly and was always seen wearing the same old tattered Army jacket.

For some reason this time, though, Mom has some unusual feelings about this man. My dad says Mom is out to help everyone whether they need it or not. Mom told us this year she wants it to be different. Mom wanted to set an example for us, and believe it or not, she convinced our dad to invite this homeless man to our house for Thanksgiving dinner.

After hearing Mom's invitation, the man said no. He told Mom the invitation was just to cure something on Mom's conscience and he doesn't want any part of it.

Mom kept after him time and time again until she gave him her special smile and he finally agreed. He then introduced himself as Dutch. He said he was just passing through and decided to stay here for a while. He didn't know how much longer he was staying. He may just move on at a moment's notice. He told her he wasn't an escaped convict or criminal or anything like that. My mom laughed and said she didn't think so, calling it "mothers intuition."

Dutch wondered why our mom never asked him about his jacket. It didn't seem a big deal to her that he was wearing a ragged old Army jacket with missing buttons. Maybe she was the lady he was looking for. He called it "Dutch's intuition."

She offered to drive Dutch over to the Salvation Army to buy whatever he thought he needed. He told her he could take a shower at the mission, but he didn't have any soap or shampoo. A quick run into the store and Mom solved that problem.

Dutch couldn't help but constantly question Mom for the reason of her help. My mom told him that moms don't need a reason to help. They can just do it. Mom told him I bet your mom is the same as me and would be more than willing to help another person in the same situation. Dutch thought about it a moment, thought about his mom, and he knew she was right.

Chapter 22

DUTCH & DANA: Thanksgiving Dinner

Finally, Thanksgiving morning came. Mom and Dad went to the area by the store to pick Dutch up, but he wasn't there. Dad began to berate Mom for her silliness and was ready to drive home.

Mom yelled, "Wait," as she saw Dutch walking quickly with a limp towards them. He still had his ragged Army coat on, but Mom never mentioned it. In his hand he held some flowers freshly picked from a lady's yard behind the store.

As he gave the flowers to my mom, Dutch said, "I had to bring something."

While at dinner we all started to ask Dutch about his life. We could tell he really didn't want to answer many questions, but he did, once he saw Mom's smile. He told us he was from a small town, his mom and dad are great people who he loved, admired and respected. He also told us that he was in the Army and had served in Vietnam. Dutch really didn't say much more than that.

When the turkey was placed on the table, Mom asked Dutch to say grace, but he started crying while doing so. There were plenty of volunteers at the dinner table who offered to help him with some of the words, but he still couldn't remember them all. It had been a very long time since he had last said it.

After dinner Dad was set to drive Dutch back to the shelter, but Mom said not until after dessert.

It was during this time that my sister Dana seemed to take a special interest in Dutch. She carefully asked him some questions about what life was like growing up in a small town since we had always lived in a big city. She asked about the difficulty of life living on the street. Dutch felt at ease but still only answered a few questions. Dutch didn't know it, but Dana had taken note of the worn lettering of his name on his Army coat.

After dessert Mom packed up some leftovers for Dutch which he gratefully accepted. She made sure everything was wrapped in aluminum foil and even gave him three slices of pumpkin pie which Dutch said was his favorite. When it was time to go I could see Dutch had tears in his eyes. He told us how this day reminded him of all the Thanksgivings he shared with his family back home. He thanked us all for our kindness. Dad, Mom and I drove Dutch back to the shelter. Mom could see Dutch waving goodbye as they were leaving. We all had tears in our eyes. Mom said Dutch was someone special, he was a mother's son and it wasn't just an accident that this all happened. Mom said there was more work we had to do to learn about Dutch. But what, when, what if he left and we never saw him again? Mom said no, we have to start now. When our mom starts getting that feeling there is no stopping her.

As soon as we returned home, Mom and Dana agreed they needed to know more about Dutch. It was now time for Mom and my sister to do what they do best—play detective. There was no time to waste. On Monday morning it all began.

Dana continued to stay in touch with Dutch, sometimes giving him food, water, an extra blanket from her bed. One time as she spoke with Dutch he told her, "You know, I have a sister just like you?"

Dana said, "I know." But he didn't hear her.

It was during the next two weeks that Mom and Dana finalized all the information about Dutch. They learned that Dutch was from a small town named Lexiville about two-hundred miles from where we lived. Dutch was a Vietnam War hero and had been wounded. Mom said, "That's why Dutch walks with a limp." The only address the Veteran's Administration had was his Lexiville address. When the VA had started sending Dutch's disability check to Lexiville his mom returned it saying that Dutch had left, and they didn't know where he had gone.

Our dad was a little bit more cautious than us. He said, "What if Dutch doesn't want to be found out? There had to be a reason he left. There's more to this story than we know." That more was exactly what my mom and I were ready to start investigating.

Mom announced to our family one cold early December day that she was going to invite Dutch for Christmas dinner. After all, Christmas is about giving and miracles.

My mom and sister were so excited to invite Dutch. When Mom asked him about coming, at first he refused. He said Christmas is about honoring the birth of baby Jesus and the giving of presents. He always honors Jesus, but he didn't have any gifts to give.

Mom just gave him one of her motherly smiles, and that was all that was needed to get Dutch to agree to come.

We were now set. We just needed to complete the final part. My mom and I knew this may be the toughest part, but we were determined.

Chapter 23

DANA: I'm Sorry to Bother You

Dana picked up the phone and dialed the number listed for what she hoped was Dutch's family in Lexiville. Her mom was at her side trying to listen. A female voice answered. Dana said, "I'm terribly sorry to bother you, but is this the residence of Dutch Blevins?"

The woman at the other end stammered and said, "Why no, it's not. I'm Dutch's mom, Mrs. Blevins, but Dutch hasn't lived here for a while now. Why do you ask? Do you know him? Are you a friend?"

Just then Dana's mom grabbed the phone out of her hand and said, "I'm Dana's mom, are you Dutch's mom?"

"Who is this? If this is a joke it's not a funny at all."

Dana's mom said, "I'll take that as a yes. Have we got something to tell you. Please sit down." By the time Dana and her mom got done telling the story of how they met Dutch, the Blevins house was full of people who heard Dutch's mom scream.

Doc Butch was at the office ready to examine Big Jim's hemorrhoids when the nurse came running in and said they found Dutch. Doc

Butch said," just stay there Jim, I'll be right back." Jim stayed there for two hours with his drawers down waiting for Dr. Butch to return. Dutch's mom agreed to send Dana some old mementos of Dutch's childhood of happier times and a photo Dutch sent when he first arrived in Vietnam. Dana agreed to send a picture of everyone seated around the dinner table at Thanksgiving which of course included Dutch. Ironically, each item arrived the same day and the women were back on the phone about what to do next. It was him. Ma Blevins went through three boxes of tissues till she stopped crying. There was her baby alive and well. Why didn't he come home? What did they do? What happened that caused Dutch to leave the way that he did?

What to do next was the biggest question each had. Ma Blevins didn't know how to handle the next step, so she spoke to Pastor Devitt. Pastor Devitt said he was pretty good at marriage counseling, but this was way out of his league. Dana, Mom and Ma Blevins discussed all the alternatives and possible outcomes.

Would Dutch be upset if he found out that Mom and Dana had called his mom? What would happen if Dutch's mom and dad traveled up to see Dutch? The hard part was, if Dutch had resolved his internal issues, then why wouldn't he return home? The other issue was, wouldn't Dutch be embarrassed if Mom and Dad saw him outside the store? Maybe they could try and arrange to see him at the mission, but no one knew when Dutch would be there.

If Dutch took off again, there was no telling where he may go, what he may do and when, if ever, they would see him again. Finally, maybe they should do nothing and wait for Dutch to decide on his own to come home. Nope, no one liked that idea at all.

Whatever decision was made had to be the right one. Since no one knew what the right decision was they all agreed they had to rely on a mother's instinct. Even if Dutch's mom and dad could see him, hug him, talk to him and tell them how much they loved him and missed him, then it would just remain up to Dutch as to what would happen next. Everyone would know that they tried their best and that was all they could do.

Now to develop a plan. My mom confirmed she had one of those maternal instincts when she invited Dutch for Thanksgiving and for Christmas, which was only a few weeks away. One place we all hoped Dutch would be was at our house for Christmas. What better day than Christmas for this hopeful reunion?

It was like God gave us Baby Jesus on Christmas and now he was giving Dutch to his mom and dad. Keeping that thought in mind, Pastor Devitt started the prayer chain at church. The whole of Lexiville was praying for something to happen on Christmas but Pastor Devitt wouldn't say what that what was. Most people thought the prayers were that Pastor Devitt could find a baby for the manger on Christmas morning.

However, Pastor Devitt already had that covered knowing that his brother's family, which included their three-year-old son, was coming for Christmas. He asked Howie's dad to build a bigger manger hoping no one would notice. Baby Jesus would just be a little bit bigger this year and if the three-year-old got out of the manger and walked around Pastor Devitt was ready to yell, "It's a miracle!" and then confess his indiscretion to his congregation.

One thing for sure was this Christmas was long to be remembered by lots of people.

The ladies only had a few weeks to scheme and plan on the events of Christmas day. First, pick up Dutch and when he walks in the house, Mom and Dad are there to surprise and greet him. No, that won't work, he may feel tricked or used and leave. Maybe, after dinner Mom and Dad call from a local hotel and Dana puts Dutch on the phone. If he is Okay, then Mom and Dad jump in their car for the quick five-minute ride. No, Ma Blevins couldn't stand the thought of not seeing Dutch in person. Even if he didn't want to see them she wanted to see him and just tell him three words: "We love you."

Finally, they decided that the best thing to do was to have Dutch's mom and dad come up the day before and check into the local hotel. Once Dutch arrived on Christmas for dinner Dad would call them and let them know he was here. After dinner, Dad would call again and they could drive over and park outside. Then we would exchange gifts and perhaps Dana could give him a few mementos from his past that his mom had sent up. Surely, he would recognize them and if all seemed well Dana would ask Dutch if he wanted to be reunited with his mom and dad. They, of course, would be waiting patiently in the car outside of our house.

Why did it seem that there had to be so much planning just for one mom to say to her one son, "We love you?" But everyone agreed this would most likely be the one and only opportunity to reunite everyone.

They agreed to all meet on Christmas in the hope of giving Dutch a Christmas he and the whole family would remember. No one knew if Dutch was better and how Dutch would take to this reunion, but Dutch's mom and dad had to see him. They thought they had lost Dutch forever.

We didn't know who was more excited, us or Dutch's mom and dad. There were daily phone calls to update each other on any new developments, but also to help prepare each other for what may happen if Dutch got upset and somehow felt betrayed by our family. We all had to remember that we didn't know the reason Dutch decided to leave and not come home after his homecoming.

As the days got closer to Christmas, Dana would stop by and drop off something for Dutch and talk to him. It seemed that they both enjoyed just talking without Dutch feeling any pressure. Eventually, Dutch asked my sister if he could tell her some personal things. He said he didn't want to burden my sister with his problems, but he felt so comfortable talking to her. Dutch talked about going to Vietnam and what he had hoped his twelve-month tour of duty would be. He then confided in her about what happened on that awful day. Dutch's eyes filled with tears as he spoke of Dennis and Ricky just lying there on the ground with blood all over them. Then of Sgt. Pikachan who rushed out to try and help Dutch but who was then shot himself and died right in front of him. These were his buddies. He promised to be there for them to protect them and he had failed. Dutch said that everyone thought he was a hero because he did what he promised his buddies he would do: help them if they got injured. He felt he wasn't a hero, but he had a hard time convincing anyone that would listen. My sister didn't say anything. She just let Dutch talk without interrupting him. This was the first time that no one interrupted him since he began to tell the events of that awful day. Someone just listened. That's really all he wanted, for someone just to listen and not try and judge him for what happened that day as to whether it was good or bad. Dutch told my sister he was so relieved that she was there to listen to him.

She told him heroes may not feel that way to themselves but, to others, it's their way of rationalizing terrible things. Like trying to make something good out of something bad. She thought there were lots of heroes in the world but the person who says the other person is a hero must truly believe it is so or else the word is meaningless. So the people that were calling Dutch a hero truly believed him to be so in their hearts but only Dutch would ever know if he rose to that status. That's what's important. She just asked Dutch not to judge others by what they thought of him on that awful day.

Dutch looked at my sister and began to sob. He told her of all the people he wronged by unfairly judging them by what they thought of him, starting with his mom and dad. How could he ever make amends to them and others? My sister said, "Dutch, I'm not sure what the answer to that is, but I'm sure there are three soldiers in heaven right now that have been trying to help you with that for a long time. Maybe it's time that you stop and just listen to what they may be telling you without interrupting them. Maybe they want to tell you what happened that day wasn't your fault. Maybe they want to tell you that in their hearts they think you are a hero, too."

Dutch hugged my sister for what seemed like an eternity. He said he had lots of thinking to do and he could never repay her for opening his mind and heart to something that had troubled him for so long. Dana told him not to worry about repaying her. Christmas was coming and lots of special things seem to happen on that day.

Dana told him to look into his heart and when the time presented itself he would know what to do. She knew that time was only a few days away.

Dana went home and told her mom about her conversation with Dutch. While they spoke it all seemed to make sense to them. Dutch had never been able to tell his whole story and with that, never able to rationalize how he could be a hero while losing three of his friends. This very simple act by Dana may have been what he needed to reconcile in his mind that which had haunted him from that awful day until today. Only time will tell, and that time was getting shorter and shorter.

Everything was planned. If all went well, Dutch's mom and dad will be at their hotel when Dutch arrives. Dad will call them and have them wait outside in their car. After Mom gives Dutch his memory gifts we tell him we have one more gift and that's when we re-introduce Dutch to his parents. We all had a family prayer during the whole week asking God to please make this go well.

Chapter 24

DANA: Now Is the Time

Christmas Day was finally here. Mom, as she did every year, reminded us about what Christmas was all about. She didn't want us to lose the thoughts of the true meaning of Christmas especially in light of all the recent events involving Dutch and his family. My dad, ever so smart, reminded Mom that Christmas was not only about the birth of Baby Jesus but exactly what was happening with Dutch and his family.

Our family had gone to church last night on Christmas Eve. We had previously invited Dutch's parents to the service at our church and they enthusiastically agreed. We could tell right away who they were, not because they were standing outside the church in the cold but by the little yellow ribbons on their coats. They looked like wonderful parents. The moms hugged and hugged, both crying without saying a word for a long time. The whole scene was repeated again by Dana and Dutch's mom. Our dad went to shake hands with Dutch's dad, but he said, "No handshake now, only a hug will do." They both had tears in their eyes as well. My Mom, Dana and Mrs. Blevins went into the church hand in hand.

Our church has a policy of visiting members being seated up front. Our family and the Blevinses took up the whole pew. Our pastor, who had been told about Dutch's story, gave a sermon on the birth of Baby Jesus and the rebirth of Christians around the world. He then asked us to pray that a new rebirth would take place between a son and his parents. Everyone stood and stretched out their hands towards Dutch's mom and dad. Our pastor began his prayers by saying, "Dear Lord, we know not why certain things happen, but we know, Lord, it is through YOU that all things occur. You gave us the best gift we could ever hope for, your son on Christmas Day. We now beseech you, o Lord, to return this brave boy to his parents, allow him to reconcile his thoughts with your help and those of the host of heavenly angels, among them three United States Army soldiers who made the supreme sacrifice for us and our country. We pray to you, Our Lord, that these men, this family and their son will find eternal peace. Amen"

As the service ended our pastor escorted the Blevinses outside. It was here that every member in attendance greeted them, hugged them and wished them well.

It was just then that the pastor brought forward an older African-American lady who was clearly in her eighties. She had asked the pastor if she could speak privately to the Blevinses. He asked them if that was okay and he introduced her as Mrs. Doretha Brown. Mrs. Brown hugged Dutch's mom and dad. She reached into her purse and took out a small cross which at one time was probably attached to a rosary. She said, "I raised my grandson from a boy and he was the best boy ever. He enlisted in the Army and was sent to Vietnam. He wrote me a letter one night and included with the letter was this cross. He told me it kept falling off the rosary and he didn't want to lose it. He said that I would know what to do with it when the time would come. He was killed that very next day while out on patrol. I never could figure how I would ever know about a time to use it but as the pastor was speaking I held in tight in my hand and I could almost hear the words, "Now is the time." Mrs. Brown opened the hand of Dutch's mom and she placed the cross into it and then closed her hand.

Tears streamed down Mrs. Blevins's cheeks. She said, "Mrs. Brown, I couldn't, I couldn't."

Mrs. Brown replied, "This is the time. Your boy will come home to you." She held Mrs. Blevins's hand closed for a minute. Mrs. Brown closed her eyes for a short time, opened them, and said, "Now is the time." With that Mrs. Brown walked a short distance to the car of her neighbor waiting to take her home and she left.

On the ride home, we passed the store where Dutch usually sat but he wasn't there. My mom said, "Well, it's late. I'm sure he's back at the mission by now. Hopefully, they can find him a bed."

On the ride back to the hotel, Mrs. Blevins held on to the cross ever so tightly saying to herself, "God, please let him still be here. Please ensure that we see him on Christmas. Through your love, Amen."

Chapter 25

DANA: Christmas Dinner

Well, hopefully this would be the Christmas to remember. As we got up and went downstairs we could see the gifts under the tree in different piles with our names on them. There was even a pile for Dutch. My mom taped an angel to one of his gifts and the wait began.

Mom told Dutch we would pick him up at two in the afternoon. Both Dana and my mom wore these beautiful red velvet dresses with a green bow in the front. My dad and I wore these silly Christmas sweaters that we wear every year, while my younger sister wore a dress with Clarise, Rudolph's girlfriend, on it. My other sister wore a sweater that said *Let it snow*. Figures, she doesn't have to shovel the sidewalk and driveway like I did.

My mom and dad drove down to the store and there he was. He had shaved and gotten a haircut but still wearing that ratty old Army jacket. When he got into our van you could smell the Aqua Velva cologne he was wearing. He had a brown bag and showed my mom these little angel statues. He said he used some of his money to buy one for each of us. This happened to be the same angel my mom had taped to one of Dutch's gifts. I don't think we ever saw him so happy.

Mom had made a Christmas ham with mashed potatoes, corn, string beans, and broccoli (there was always lots of leftovers of the broccoli).

After dinner we gathered around the Christmas tree to pass out the gifts. Dutch received, some new shirts, sweaters, even some underwear. Dutch, with a red face, told us how grateful he was. He said thank you for each gift and then announced he had a gift for me and my three sisters. Then he started to cry.

He reached into his pocket and gave my sister a button that was once on his Army jacket. He did the same with each of us, giving us a button from the Army jackets of his fallen comrades. It was finally time, thought Dutch.

Mom had always offered to sew buttons onto his jacket, but he always politely refused. He told us that he hoped one day we will know the significance of the button as a special way of remembering him and some very special friends.

He really didn't think he would ever see us again. We all initially refused to accept the buttons, but he insisted we keep them. "How will you close your Army coat?" my sister said. Dutch said he could still tie his Army coat with a rope to keep out the winter chill.

Chapter 26

DANA: Dutch's Gift

Dana said, "Oh Look! In the back of the tree there are still a few more presents for Dutch." It was now time for Dutch to get his real presents. We all held our breath. The first present given to Dutch by Dana was a watch, not a new watch, but a watch that has seen much better days.

Dutch looked at the watch as tears began to run down his cheeks. He said to Dana, "Where did you get this? This was a present from my parents when I graduated grade school." My dad excused himself and went into the bedroom and called Dutch's parents to come over. Dutch waited for him to return and opened the next gift and more tears streamed down his face. Dutch looked at the childlike drawings every parent puts on the refrigerator. "These were drawings I did at school, all of them." The words *I love you* were written throughout the papers. "How could you have gotten these? They must be over forty years old. I don't understand..."

Time for the last gift. It was an envelope with a letter. The letter was from his mother and father.

He recognized his mother's handwriting. The letter contained only a few words: "We love you and we have never stopped loving you...ever."

His tears were matched only by his mother's and father's as my mom opened the front door to let them in. They all looked at each other for a moment until Dutch's mom ran and hugged him for what seemed like an eternity. Then it was Dad's turn. He told us, "I never cry but if there ever was a reason to cry this is it." I could still see Mrs. Blevins's hand clenched tightly around the cross she had received at church earlier. Dutch sat between his mother and dad who continually just looked at him and hugged him.

It was then that we heard their story of Dutch. *Dutch* was a nickname for their son as he was known around the neighborhood in Lexiville. Dutch had been drafted into the Army and was sent to Vietnam at nineteen years old, directly after boot camp and medic school. Because of the things that happened there he returned home with a severe case of PTSD. Dutch could no longer accept society's rules as he was forced to do in the Army. Mrs. Blevins said that they received a note saying he was leaving and would no longer be a burden to them. They searched and searched with no luck. They finally gave up the search. But they never gave up loving him.

Well, Mom brought out the homemade Christmas pies and coffee for everyone. We all talked about our families and how anxious everyone in Lexiville was to see Dutch. The conversation lasted well past midnight. Finally, Dutch's dad said, "Son, we don't want to make the same mistake as last time. Do you want to go back home? I mean, only if you are and you feel ready to. If not, that's okay but could you at least leave us your address?"

Everyone laughed and Dutch said, "I'm ready to go home, Mom and Dad."

There were so many tears in the room as Dutch's mom and dad put on their coats ready to take Dutch home to see his brother and sisters and their children. Dutch hugged and thanked every one of us.

One of my sisters said, "Mr. Dutch, do you want your button back?"

"No," Dutch said. "This jacket means more to me than any other item I have. Many of my friends were killed wearing a jacket just like this. I wanted you to have a part of something that was the most important thing to me in the world. Please keep them and remember everything your mom and dad did, and especially your sister, Dana. Please remember the importance of the sacrifices each of those buttons represent."

Dutch turned to Dana. "How did you find out who I was and find my parents?"

Dana said, "Well, I'm the daughter of a very famous policeman and I saw your name on your Army coat, and although I could barely make it out, I did, and I worked with Miss Marcy Mills and Sammi Lowe of the Veterans Administration and some volunteer organizations. We all worked very hard to figure out who you were and then we contacted your mom and dad and, well, you know the rest."

"I know, and thank you so much." With that, he asked if he could have a pair of scissors. He cut his name off the jacket and handed it to Dana. He said, "You are my angel, please take this with my name and keep it and think of me as I will do with you and the rest of your wonderful family. I can never repay you for your kindness. I had to sort through a lot of things in my mind, but I know Dana helped me do that when we spoke a few days back."

Dutch's dad asked everybody to stand in a circle and hold hands to pray. He said, "Heavenly Father, you know I am not one to ask you for things. As a matter of fact, the only thing I think I ever asked for was the return of Dutch. Now, I hope you'll forget some of the bad things I said a few times, but I guess that's just what dads have to do: pray and hope. You know 'cause you're a dad who sent his son to us. Well, me and Ma did lots of both, praying and hoping. If it wasn't for the kind family in this room who knows if we would ever have seen our son again? Amen." And then to Dutch: If there is anything I can ever do to help you, just say the word. And son, when they needed you in the war they would yell "Doc up." If you need me anywhere, just let me hear in my heart "Dad up" and you'll find me right in the front 'cause that's where I'll be heading to help you with whatever you need."

Shortly after midnight Dutch and his mom and dad were just as plum tired as us. While my dad insisted they stay over at our house they said they didn't want to impose any more. They would go back to the hotel, get a good night's sleep and head back to Lexiville in the morning. We all said our goodbyes which seemed never-ending. Dutch gave each of us a special hug. We knew that something very special had just happened and we would carry this through the rest of our lives. We didn't know if Dutch needed any more help. What he had gone through was horrific but we all knew his mom and dad and a whole town would be there to support him.

We learned that in the morning, Ma Blevins had called her other children to tell them Dutch was coming home. They insisted no special homecoming other than hugs and kisses. That could come later, but only if Dutch agreed.

When they all arrived back home a group of neighbors were standing outside of the house.

When Dutch got out of the car they began singing "America the Beautiful" and then, as fast as they had started, they all yelled "Welcome home, Dutch!" and with that they left and went back home. Dutch didn't know there were still a few more tears inside him but out they came. Even more when he went inside and was greeted by his brothers and sisters, aunts and uncles. Everybody in the family was there.

What a special day that was. Slowly, Dutch's story made its way through Lexiville. About a month later the town decided that they wanted to give Dutch the homecoming that had been cut so short the last time. However, this time Dutch and his mom would plan the event.

It was on a clear crisp January Saturday afternoon when Dutch felt it was time to thank the town for their support. There stood Dutch in his dress uniform with lots of medals hanging from his chest. He stood at the face of the gazebo and addressed just about everyone in Lexiville. Of course, my family wouldn't have missed it for the world. Dutch made sure that everyone knew our names and, briefly, what happened. The whole town then adopted us as Lexivillians. I think that was the term they used.

Dutch then stood at the podium in front of the microphone to speak from some notes he had made. He spoke about friendship, faith, friends, love and honor and then he made a special request that everyone say a prayer for all the soldiers who had died and their families who had to carry on without them. He said he had much more to say but he couldn't as he was getting choked on each word. Everyone understood, and they applauded Dutch.

It was then that Pap and other members of the VFW had a ceremonial raising of the flag. They handed the triangular-shaped folded flag to Dutch and he attached it to the cable and raised it while everyone sang "The Star-Spangled Banner." Then every person in Lexiville who had served in the armed forces, their family, or who had lost a friend or family member in a war, gathered in front of Dutch. Grandma Joan was in the very front. They stood at attention and Pap said in a loud, clear voice: "Hand salute!" They each saluted the American Flag and then turned and saluted Dutch. Dutch smartly returned their salute at which Pap sounded off with "At ease." Dutch then had the opportunity to greet everyone in attendance.

Dutch saw a young boy in the crowd and recognized him from the first homecoming. He felt absolutely terrible about the incident and asked his mom to fill him in with information about the boy. Dutch walked over to Howie. He extended his hand and said, "Howie, I hope you will give me the honor of shaking my hand." Howie immediately extended his hand and they shook hands for what seemed like an eternity. Dutch bent down and said, "I'm told that you and I may share something special. We are both being called heroes. Now, if we are indeed heroes we have a special duty to honor, protect and help wherever we can. I think you and I would make a pretty good team of heroes. What do you think, Howie?"

"Sure, Mr. Dutch" said Howie.

Dutch bent down and said, "Howie, I'm told that heroes get some form of recognition for what they did. I know you have your baseball and what a great remembrance that is. I can only apologize for the way I acted before. I would like to give you something special that some heroes have. He then unpinned one his medals and pinned it to Howie's shirt.

Howie looked at the medal, looked at Dutch, and then the medal in awe. Howie took one step back and saluted Dutch. Dutch returned the salute and then hugged Lexiville's other hero. Dutch said, "Now let's take a look at that ball and tell me everything that happened."

Chapter 27

DUTCH: Dutch Keeps His Promise

Dutch had made a promise to himself that if he was ever able he would visit the families of Sgt. Pikachan, Dennis and Ricky. It was mid-April when he and Dana tracked down the last of their addresses. He decided to call first to make sure he was welcome. In all three of the calls the families told Dutch he was more than welcome to visit, and they were anxious to hear what happened that day. There were lots of tears, hugs and prayers at each of the family's homes. Each of the families had the gold star provided by the Army in their front window.

Dutch apologized that he couldn't do more to help but they all agreed that it was God's will. He felt that he could feel the presence of each of the soldiers at their homes. The families shared pictures and remembrances about their loved ones with Dutch. Upon leaving they all made him feel like he was part of their family too.

There was one final thing that Dutch needed to do. Only then could he be completely at peace with himself. His last visit was to Arlington National Cemetery where he visited the graves of each of his three comrades. He found much solace and comfort when he stopped at their gravesites. He laid a flower on each of the tombstones and ended his visit with a salute.

Dutch then traveled across the bridge to the Vietnam Veterans Memorial. There he traced the names of each of his friends. Although he was not in uniform several individuals approached him and called him *brother*. They hugged and spoke about their experiences. He asked one of the veterans how they could tell that he served in Vietnam. This man replied, "We all know a fellow brother when we see him and don't worry, you'll be able to tell too." Dutch made it a point to visit the memorial whenever he could. They were right; in time he could sense another veteran's grief and would try to speak with.

Chapter 28

DANA: The Worst Call Ever

After about two years Dutch started feeling ill. It seemed like he had lost all his stamina. He stayed in bed longer and it was painful when he moved his arms and legs. Dutch traveled to the VA hospital where he was admitted for a round of testing. When all the tests were completed and evaluated the doctor met with Dutch and his parents. The prognosis was bad. Dutch was suffering from a debilitating disease most likely caused by a chemical defoliant which had been spayed in parts of Vietnam.

Dutch would soon lose the use of his extremities with death to follow. The doctor advised Dutch that he had less than two months to live. While his mom and dad cried Dutch attempted to console them by reminding them what a great life they gave him. He asked them to be an inspiration to other parents of sick veterans and help them in any way. The doctor advised Dutch it would be best to be admitted to the hospital where his daily hospice care could be provided by the doctors and nursing staff.

Dutch spoke with his parents privately and thanked the doctor for his generous offer, but he would return to Lexiville to die in the town where he was raised. He was sure that Doc Butch could provide whatever medical necessities were needed to make him comfortable.

Dutch called my mom and told her about the medical prognosis. My mom almost fainted. She gathered us all around the phone and Dutch asked to speak to each of us individually. As the crying started the phone was passed to each family member. Dutch said something different to each of us.

The following week we drove to Lexiville to see Dutch one last time. He had lost lots of weight and looked so tired. Then he saw our mom's smile which lit up the room. Dutch said he would always remember that smile. We each gave Dutch a kiss on the cheek and thanked him for being such a special part of our lives.

Two days later that we got the terrible news that Dutch had passed away. Ma Blevins said she was sure that Dutch held on till he could see us one last time. How we wished that last time could go on for an eternity.

Dutch's viewing would be held at the Heavenly Rest Funeral Home. There was an honor guard of four Army soldiers in their dress uniforms who stood at the four corners of the casket. Dutch was laid out in his dress uniform with all his medals with one conspicuously missing.

The mystery was solved as one young man along with his parents entered the funeral home wearing a suit with a medal on the lapel.

As he approached the coffin he knelt and said The Lord's Prayer and then reached into his pocket and took out a baseball and placed it in the coffin. Howie said, "From one hero to another: Goodbye, my friend."

My mom and I, along with our entire family, walked up together while we held hands. Who would have known that the man we saw before us would have played such a profound part of our lives? It's hard to believe, given what he went through and the manner in which he tried to cope with it, that anything positive could ever have come of this. I looked at my mom as tears streamed down her face and my dad who held her tightly. Our family getting involved in Dutch's life all started because of a mother's smile. It was her smile that disarmed Dutch to believe in her. We'll never know for sure if Dutch had ever figured out that we had a plan. I guess its fair to say that it really developed along the way. As we looked around the room and saw literally hundreds of people inside and outside the funeral home whose lives had crossed the path of a very special man. We all felt blessed that day.

Dutch's life and death affected so many people. As I gazed again into the coffin I spied something I had overlooked before. There, in Dutch's folded hands, was a little cross, the one given to Dutch's mom by Mrs. Brown at our church on Christmas Eve. She said it was time for Dutch to come home and she was right.

Dutch's mom came to me and said, "Dana, can you come with me for a minute? I need your help." She led me to a chair that had a bag on it. We picked up the bag and walked back to Dutch's coffin. Dutch's mom and I took out his green Army jacket and folded it neatly and placed at Dutch's feet. On top of it we placed that piece of old white rope he used to tie it with. With that we said our goodbyes to the hero that lay before us. Tomorrow this hero will be laid to rest among so many others.

Chapter 29

POPS: Dutch's Final Resting Place

The Army had granted the request of the Blevins family to allow Dutch to be buried at Arlington National Cemetery with full military honors.

The following morning, Pastor Devitt gave a brief sermon talking about death and life. It was so hard to concentrate on what he was saying. Shortly after that, Dutch was carried by the military honor guard to the waiting hearse. Their steps were measured, and they moved in perfect unison as they carried Dutch. With the greatest of care, they placed the coffin into the hearse and rolled it in. Then they stood erect and slowly raised hands in their final salute to Dutch. A different honor guard would meet Dutch at Arlington National Cemetery and assist with the remaining part of his burial. A Lexiville police car started the procession with its red lights flashing. The line of cars following in a row seemed to go on and on. As we approached an intersection we could see that the police blocked the traffic until the entire procession of cars passed. It was a forty-five-minute drive to the cemetery and no one said a word. Upon our arrival we were directed to a site to wait a brief time. It was then that the hearse came forward and a new honor guard came forward to take Dutch from the hearse to the burial site. We could now see his coffin was draped with the American flag. Again, with measured steps the honor guard moved forward placing the casket on the silver supports on top of the grave. An Army Chaplain spoke about Dutch, recounting his youth and upbringing in Lexiville. He talked about Dutch's heroic actions on that awful day. He talked about love, kindness and how heroism is so broadly defined but not in the case of Dutch. He told us that heroism could be defined as what took place on the battlefield and what took place on a ball field.

We four to whom Dutch had given the buttons on Christmas each held them tightly in our hand. We squeezed ever so hard as the rifle salute was fired. "Ready, fire! Ready, fire! Ready, fire!" And after each command of fire, the guns were shot. Then we heard the slow mournful sound of "Taps" played by an Army bugler. It almost sounded like there was an echo at the top of a hill.

The honor guard moved forward and removed the American flag from Dutch's coffin and briskly folded it in a triangular shape with the sea of blue stars facing outward. One of the soldiers grasped the flag to his heart and marched to an Army officer who received the flag, then approached Dutch's mom and said, "On behalf of the President of the United States and a grateful nation, please accept this flag as a symbol of our appreciation for your loved one's honorable and faithful service."

At that point, Dutch's mom reached back and stood up and asked Dana, who was standing behind her, to walk around in front. She then handed the flag to Dana. Dana said, "I can't take this flag, it belongs to you and your family."

Dutch's mom said, "Dutch talked to me about it and we both agreed that you should have it. It is you who brought our Dutch home to us. None of this would have ever happened were it not for you and your family. We love you all and will never forget all you have done."

Back in Lexiville, Pap and the old veterans met in the town square at the gazebo, lowered the flag to half-staff and saluted.

Dana wept, and the tears began to cover the flag as she held it to her heart. The four buttons we all held told a story none of us will ever forget. The baseball placed in Dutch's casket by Howie the hero will remain with him through eternity.

Everyone who knows this story knows it by his name—Dutch. That man had a name and a story. Then there was Howie. These were two heroes whose stories are told simply by four buttons and a baseball.

About the Author

Dennis Guzy is retired from a thirty-two-year career in law enforcement. He and his wife, Marilyn, adopt and care for senior rescue dogs in their Central Pennsylvania home. They have two children and three grandchildren. This is his first book.

Printed in Great Britain
by Amazon

20030891R00068